Twenty Fathoms Down

SELECTED FICTION WORKS BY
L. RON HUBBARD

FANTASY
The Case of the Friendly Corpse

Death's Deputy

Fear

The Ghoul

The Indigestible Triton

Slaves of Sleep & The Masters of Sleep

Typewriter in the Sky

The Ultimate Adventure

SCIENCE FICTION
Battlefield Earth

The Conquest of Space

The End Is Not Yet

Final Blackout

The Kilkenny Cats

The Kingslayer

The Mission Earth Dekalogy*

Ole Doc Methuselah

To the Stars

ADVENTURE
The Hell Job series

WESTERN
Buckskin Brigades

Empty Saddles

Guns of Mark Jardine

Hot Lead Payoff

A full list of L. Ron Hubbard's
novellas and short stories is provided at the back.

*Dekalogy—a group of ten volumes

L. RON HUBBARD

Twenty Fathoms Down

GALAXY
PRESS

Published by
Galaxy Press, LLC
7051 Hollywood Boulevard, Suite 200
Hollywood, CA 90028

Printed in the United States of America.

ISBN-10 1-59212-251-5
ISBN-13 978-1-59212-251-6

Library of Congress Control Number: 2007927534

Contents

Stories from Pulp Fiction's Golden Age

AND it *was* a golden age.

The 1930s and 1940s were a vibrant, seminal time for a gigantic audience of eager readers, probably the largest per capita audience of readers in American history. The magazine racks were chock-full of publications with ragged trims, garish cover art, cheap brown pulp paper, low cover prices—and the most excitement you could hold in your hands.

"Pulp" magazines, named for their rough-cut, pulpwood paper, were a vehicle for more amazing tales than Scheherazade could have told in a million and one nights. Set apart from higher-class "slick" magazines, printed on fancy glossy paper with quality artwork and superior production values, the pulps were for the "rest of us," adventure story after adventure story for people who liked to *read*. Pulp fiction authors were no-holds-barred entertainers—real storytellers. They were more interested in a thrilling plot twist, a horrific villain or a white-knuckle adventure than they were in lavish prose or convoluted metaphors.

The sheer volume of tales released during this wondrous golden age remains unmatched in any other period of literary history—hundreds of thousands of published stories in over nine hundred different magazines. Some titles lasted only an issue or two; many magazines succumbed to paper shortages during World War II, while others endured for decades yet. Pulp fiction remains as a treasure trove of stories you can read, stories you can love, stories you can remember. The stories were driven by plot and character, with grand heroes, terrible villains, beautiful damsels (often in distress), diabolical plots, amazing places, breathless romances. The readers wanted to be taken beyond the mundane, to live adventures far removed from their ordinary lives—and the pulps rarely failed to deliver.

In that regard, pulp fiction stands in the tradition of all memorable literature. For as history has shown, good stories are much more than fancy prose. William Shakespeare, Charles Dickens, Jules Verne, Alexandre Dumas—many of the greatest literary figures wrote their fiction for the readers, not simply literary colleagues and academic admirers. And writers for pulp magazines were no exception. These publications reached an audience that dwarfed the circulations of today's short story magazines. Issues of the pulps were scooped up and read by over thirty million avid readers each month.

Because pulp fiction writers were often paid no more than a cent a word, they had to become prolific or starve. They also had to write aggressively. As Richard Kyle, publisher and editor of *Argosy*, the first and most long-lived of the pulps, so pointedly explained: "The pulp magazine writers, the best of them, worked for markets that did not write for critics or attempt to satisfy timid advertisers. Not having to answer to anyone other than their readers, they wrote about human beings on the edges of the unknown, in those new lands the future would explore. They wrote for what we would become, not for what we had already been."

Some of the more lasting names that graced the pulps include H. P. Lovecraft, Edgar Rice Burroughs, Robert E. Howard, Max Brand, Louis L'Amour, Elmore Leonard, Dashiell Hammett, Raymond Chandler, Erle Stanley Gardner, John D. MacDonald, Ray Bradbury, Isaac Asimov, Robert Heinlein—and, of course, L. Ron Hubbard.

In a word, he was among the most prolific and popular writers of the era. He was also the most enduring—hence this series—and certainly among the most legendary. It all began only months after he first tried his hand at fiction, with L. Ron Hubbard tales appearing in *Thrilling Adventures, Argosy, Five-Novels Monthly, Detective Fiction Weekly, Top-Notch, Texas Ranger, War Birds, Western Stories,* even *Romantic Range.* He could write on any subject, in any genre, from jungle explorers to deep-sea divers, from G-men and gangsters, cowboys and flying aces to mountain climbers, hard-boiled detectives and spies. But he really began to shine when he turned his talent to science fiction and fantasy of which he authored nearly fifty novels or novelettes to forever change the shape of those genres.

Following in the tradition of such famed authors as Herman Melville, Mark Twain, Jack London and Ernest Hemingway, Ron Hubbard actually lived adventures that his own characters would have admired—as an ethnologist among primitive tribes, as prospector and engineer in hostile

ix

climes, as a captain of vessels on four oceans. He even wrote a series of articles for *Argosy,* called "Hell Job," in which he lived and told of the most dangerous professions a man could put his hand to.

Finally, and just for good measure, he was also an accomplished photographer, artist, filmmaker, musician and educator. But he was first and foremost a *writer,* and that's the L. Ron Hubbard we come to know through the pages of this volume.

This library of Stories from the Golden Age presents the best of L. Ron Hubbard's fiction from the heyday of storytelling, the Golden Age of the pulp magazines. In these eighty volumes, readers are treated to a full banquet of 153 stories, a kaleidoscope of tales representing every imaginable genre: science fiction, fantasy, western, mystery, thriller, horror, even romance—action of all kinds and in all places.

Because the pulps themselves were printed on such inexpensive paper with high acid content, issues were not meant to endure. As the years go by, the original issues of every pulp from *Argosy* through *Zeppelin Stories* continue crumbling into brittle, brown dust. This library preserves the L. Ron Hubbard tales from that era, presented with a distinctive look that brings back the nostalgic flavor of those times.

L. Ron Hubbard's Stories from the Golden Age has something for every taste, every reader. These tales will return you to a time when fiction was good clean entertainment and the most fun a kid could have on a rainy afternoon or the best thing an adult could enjoy after a long day at work.

Pick up a volume, and remember what reading is supposed to be all about. Remember curling up with a *great story*.

—Kevin J. Anderson

KEVIN J. ANDERSON *is the author of more than ninety critically acclaimed works of speculative fiction, including* The Saga of Seven Suns, *the continuation of the* Dune Chronicles *with Brian Herbert, and his* New York Times *bestselling novelization of L. Ron Hubbard's* Ai! Pedrito!

Twenty Fathoms Down

CHAPTER ONE

The Stowaway

HAWK RIDLEY picked up the yellow sheets of parchment, folded them into a compact bundle, and placed the whole in the pouch that hung around his neck. "I'll take charge of these things now that we're under weigh," he said. "If they're worth a hundred thousand dollars to Chuck Mercer, they're worth ten times that to us."

Captain Steve Gregory gave the receding lights of New York a parting squint and then glanced out across the rain-spattered decks of the *Stingaree*.

"Judging from past events," he remarked, "I'd say those things are a good death warrant. Believe me, Hawk, I look for plenty of trouble down off Haiti. It's my guess that that old galleon has more than a few million in gold aboard her."

Hawk's lean, bronzed face relaxed in a grin and he shifted his lanky weight against the charting table. Youth and the anticipation of adventure made his sea blue eyes sparkle. The captain looked at his chief and then his own round, sunburned face also relaxed.

"Doesn't worry you much, does it, Hawk?" continued Gregory. "You'd think that a diver like you would be having the shakes. Why, boy, you don't even know what Mercer may have in store for us! Twenty fathoms down is pretty darn—"

"Stokey Watts and I will take care of twenty fathoms,"

Hawk interrupted. "All you've got to do is to get this tub of rust down into the Windward Passage off Haiti. We'll do the rest. We're going to get that treasure this time, Greg, and don't you forget it!"

Gregory laughed suddenly. "Anyway, you sure gave Al Mercer a send-off! I'll be a long time forgetting the way that boy took the dive when you threw him down the gangway tonight!"

"He did look funny, didn't he?" agreed Hawk. "But any time anybody points a gun at me and demands that I hand over anything, I'm apt to get cross. They've tried to buy these charts, then steal them, and then to put us out of commission. Lord only knows what they'll do next."

The *Stingaree*'s captain was suddenly sober. "Yes, the Lord only knows. I'm looking for trouble, Hawk. Not that I want it, but I know it's coming. Al and Chuck made enough sly remarks as to what would happen if we so much as weighed anchor to go after that bullion."

Hawk looked out across the sea as though his keen eyes could pierce the rain-drenched dark and see the coast which was their goal.

"They're certainly after us," he said.

Well, it was enough that the salvage ship was at last putting out for the West Indies with her diving equipment and competent crew. The sailing had been delayed day by day for two weeks. Minor troubles, just serious enough to rasp on the men's nerves, had occurred with relentless regularity, and the blame had been laid—not without reason—at the

4

door of Ocean Salvage, a rival firm managed by Chuck and Al Mercer.

The bridge itself gave enough indication that trouble of one sort or another was anticipated. Racks of rifles climbed up the after side of the chart room, and ammunition boxes were carefully stowed so as to be handy, yet out of the way.

Even the engines below decks seemed to throb in a subdued, cautious key, as though they, too, sensed danger. The rain, whispering against the steel plates of the decks, added to the feeling of danger ahead.

But though Hawk Ridley and Gregory were keyed up against surprise, the seeming apparition that appeared in the open doorway gave them a shock. For, of all things they expected to see on a salvage ship, a slender, lovely girl in a bedraggled wedding dress was the last.

She stood with one hand resting upon the side of the doorway, gazing into the room with half-frightened, half-pleading eyes.

At first, Hawk felt as though someone had swept away the world about him to replace it with one of fantasy. Then he had only eyes for the delicate beauty of her face.

It was the girl who broke the silence.

"I suppose," she faltered, "that you'll set me ashore, now that you know I'm here."

"What the—?" came Gregory's gasp. "What are you doing on the *Stingaree*?"

Hawk managed to collect himself enough to speak. "Come on in," he said. "You'll catch your death of cold in those wet things." He stepped forward and held out a hand to help her over the door jamb.

Hesitantly the girl entered. She stood there looking about. Hawk pulled a chair to the side of the steam radiator and motioned for her to sit down. With a sigh, she spread out the wet white satin of her gown and seated herself.

Her lips quivered as she looked up at Hawk. "What do you do with stowaways, Mr. Ridley? It's not an awful crime, is it?"

"Stowaway?" said Hawk. "Do you mean—that is, you're a stowaway?"

"What's it look like?" interjected Gregory, regaining his dignity as master of a ship. "Who are you, anyway?"

The girl looked at Hawk, as though he might prove her ally. "I won't be any trouble to you. Really I won't be any trouble. I knew you were sailing and I had to come. There wasn't anything else I could do, was there?" She sent the question straight up at Hawk.

Hawk was once more in a trance and he did not seem to hear her words. She continued:

"You see, I'm Vick—Fredericka Stanton, Charles Stanton's daughter. I had to come. There wasn't any other way!"

Gregory's eyes went hard. "C.H. Stanton, eh? You mean that you, C.H. Stanton's daughter, have got the unmitigated crust to come on board this ship when we're putting out to sea? I happen to know that Stanton and the Mercers do business together. That lets you out, understand?" Gregory turned to Hawk. "Guess we'll have to put her ashore, Hawk."

The girl gasped. "No, oh, no! You can't do that! You can't

put me ashore. I have money in New York. I'll pay you well to take me with you. Just as soon as we get back, I'll pay you in cash! You *must* let me go!"

"Yeah?" snapped Gregory. "Listen here, little lady, I see your game. Mercer wants an agent aboard this ship and he got Stanton to send you along. He thought you could play on our sympathy with some cock-and-bull story, eh? Well, he's wrong, and you're wrong! You're going to get off the *Stingaree* just as soon as I can place you within launch distance of the beach!"

"Keep still!" Hawk said so suddenly that Gregory jumped. "Can't you see the girl is shot to pieces? Who's running this ship, anyway?"

The girl gave him a grateful, relieved glance. "I knew you'd help me, Mr. Ridley. I've heard so much about you, and I know you're decent. That's why I came. I knew that you were the only person I could appeal to. All the others—" Tears brightened in her eyes.

"Don't let a pretty girl wreck you!" Gregory cried. "Can't you see that Mercer sent her aboard to get the charts or tip him off? It's a grandstand play, Hawk!"

Hawk looked at him with eyes chill as ice. "Some of these days, Captain, you're going to put in your two cents just once too often. This girl is cold and wet and miserable. Let her alone!"

The captain brushed a nervous hand across his brow. "You're like that, Hawk. Every time I try to hand out some advice you get stubborn. The answer's as plain as the nose on your face. This girl's a plant! Just because she's pretty—"

"Go tell the steward," said Hawk coldly, "to make up a spare cabin. And tell him to get this girl some dry clothes and something to eat. And," he paused for effect, "if I catch one man on this ship bothering her, I'll give him a good stiff jolt to remember me by."

When Gregory had gone the girl looked up at Hawk with a faint smile of gratitude.

"I knew you'd understand," she said. "There wasn't any place for me to go but here—so I came."

Hawk leaned back against the charting table. "Maybe I'm crazy, Miss Stanton, and maybe it does look funny, your coming aboard in a wet wedding dress, but somehow I'd stake everything I've got on you. I don't know why you're here, but I know that you've a good reason, and I'm not such a roughneck that I'd let a lady down."

Vick Stanton's smile was radiant. "And I was almost ready to believe that chivalry was dead!" she said.

CHAPTER TWO

The Death Warrant

THREE men leaned against the charting table on the bridge of the anchored *Stingaree*. Their chins were rested on their palms and their eyes were intent on the shaded tracings on an aged yellow parchment chart.

Across the room, on a leather transom, sat Vick Stanton, clothed in white sailor pants, a seaman's blouse and tennis shoes. Wisps of shining blond hair escaped from under the yachting cap she wore, and in spite of the masculine garb, she looked appealingly feminine. From time to time her eyes wandered out across the blue water of the Windward Passage, which terminated in the harsh brown landscape that was Haiti, but her glance always returned to Hawk Ridley.

On Hawk's right was Gregory, and on his left was Stokey Watts, his assistant diver. Stokey had a certain chunky stolidness that belied the adventurous nature of his chosen work, and from his manner one might have guessed that he was cautious, rather than venturesome.

He traced a stubby finger down the coastline of Haiti, and then tapped the red X that stood out boldly against the aged yellow scroll.

"This must be the spot," he said. "It checks with the coastline to a hair."

"I think so, too," said Captain Gregory, "but you never can tell. Those Spaniards weren't so accurate about their charts in those days."

"Maybe not," said Stokey. "But it seems to me that if I was a captain of a gold-bearing galleon and I lost my ship on a reef, I'd mark it accurate, whether I was Spanish or Greek. Nobody is going to make a mistake in plotting the position of three tons or so of gold."

"We're right," Hawk assured them. "The only thing I'm worrying about is whether the ship is on a hard bottom, or whether she's gone to pieces and sunk in the ooze. If she's on hard coral, she might have drifted quite a ways from the spot. See here. This is the reef the galleon hit, and here is where she floated off and sank. They didn't know how deep it was there, and we're not sure that our drag is in the wreck. But I'm betting that I can locate the thing in a day."

"Even if she's gone to pieces," said Stokey, "this construction map you got in Spain will tell us what part of the ship to look under. Y'know, come to think of it, Hawk, this position chart isn't much good unless it's backed up with the plans of the galleon."

"You're not the only one that knows that," Hawk grinned. "Mercer was hellbent on getting this chart." He traced the outline of the wolf's head of Haiti all the way around and came back to the cross. "Anybody with a few weeks to look around could find the thing."

Stokey stepped back and brushed back a lock of red hair. "Well, there's no use standing here all day chinning about it. Who's going to take the first dive, Hawk, you or me?"

10

"I will." Hawk folded up the charts and thrust them into his shirt front. "Go on forward and rout out the crews. I'll be there as soon as you get the gear set up." He walked out to the deck and stood for a moment gazing across the unbelievably blue water. He was about to walk on down the superstructure when he felt the light touch of a hand on his arm. Vick.

"All set?" she said.

"And rarin' to go!" Hawk pointed down. "In twenty minutes I'll be walking around a hundred feet beneath you."

Vick's smile faded. "There isn't any danger to it, is there? No sharks, or anything like that?"

Hawk laughed down at her. "Maybe, and maybe not. Sometimes a shark makes a pass at you, but not often, and as far as these waters go, there's little else to worry about—that is, that a diver can't avoid if he uses his head. It's pretty light down there on a bright day like this."

"You know, Hawk, you never asked me any questions on the way down. I hope you don't think that I . . . that . . ."

"What's the need of questions?" Hawk smiled. "I never do any prying into other people's business. You came aboard in trouble, and unless you wanted to tell me the story, it wasn't necessary."

The troubled look in her eyes was still there. "I heard some of the men talking, and they think I'm in Mercer's pay just because my father is Charles Stanton. Do you think so?"

Taken aback by her directness, Hawk laid both hands on the rail and looked out toward the mountains of Haiti. "Don't worry about it, Vick. I don't think you'd double-cross me."

She smiled at that and raised her head in sudden decision.

11

"There's one thing I know that you should know. Maybe it will help you. I heard that Chuck Mercer was fixing up some different kind of boat to come down here and put you out of business. You can take that for what it's worth to you. I don't know anything more than that—and that was just a rumor."

Hawk regarded her soberly. "Then it's pretty certain that Ocean Salvage is going to make a fight for the bullion?"

Vick looked down at the steel plates of the deck, then back at Hawk. "Yes, pretty certain."

Before he could say more, Hawk heard Stokey's call from the forward well deck, and he turned away, to clatter down toward the array of diving equipment which had been laid out below.

Seating himself on a three-legged stool, Hawk allowed his "bears" to pull the rubber and canvas diving suit over his legs. The two men worked silently and quickly at the lacings, and then helped him to his feet, so that he could pull on the rest of the outfit.

Vick stood by the landing stage and watched the procedure with critical eyes, and when Hawk looked up she gave him a smile.

The two sixteen-pound shoes had been strapped on, the eighty pounds of lead belts were in place, the corselet had been screwed down tight over the bib, and Hawk was inspecting the helmet one of his bears held out to him.

Vick came and stood beside Hawk. "Let me put your helmet on for you—maybe it will bring you some good luck," she said.

"Go to it," Hawk laughed. "In the old days, ladies set a knight's helmet in place, didn't they?"

With fingers quick and sure, Vick slid the copper globe over his head and fitted it securely on the glinting corselet. In a few seconds all the dogs were expertly battened, and the dress was complete.

"Well done!" Hawk applauded through the plate-glass window at the helmet's front. "You must know something about this game, Vick."

She shook her head, and stood back to let him step up on the lowering stage.

A winch creaked and groaned as it took in enough cable to swing the stage over the rail, and then, amid a cloud of steam, lowered the platform down to the level of the sea.

As he went toward the water, Hawk flexed his arms stiffly and looked at the weather-beaten side of the *Stingaree* as it crept past his window. His thoughts were on the task before him. Down below on a sandy floor was the wreck of a galleon centuries old, and in that wreck three tons of gold bullion. . . .

The sight of crude lettering on the side of the ship snapped across his thoughts. He felt dizzy, as though he had been spun about. For there, written in white chalk on the steel plates, were the ugly words, "Death at Twenty Fathoms!"

An involuntary gasp escaped Hawk's compressed lips. The import and the source of the legend were plain. Someone had written that warning to frighten the *Stingaree* away from the task of salvaging the gold.

"Haul me back!" Hawk snapped into the telephone.

13

The startled winch operator followed the order, and in a moment the stage swayed close to the side of the rail where the crew stood, puzzled and questioning. Hawk waved to Stokey to board the platform, and Stokey obeyed with all the alacrity of which his chunky body was capable.

Through his opened helmet window, Hawk said but a single word: "Look!" And he pointed at the writing which had been invisible from the deck.

Stokey read the words with bugging eyes. "What the devil! Who's responsible for that?"

"Mercer," said Hawk without hesitation. "He put that there while we were still in New York and we never noticed it until now. I wanted you to see it, so you wouldn't be jarred out of your boots by it tomorrow."

"You don't suppose there's anything behind that, do you?" Stokey was plainly shaken. "Maybe a trap's been laid, or something like that."

"Don't be foolish!" said Hawk. "That only means that we're going to have to keep a sharp lookout for boats. Tell Gregory that if he sees any strange craft around here to let me know immediately, and to take every precaution necessary to keep them away from us."

"You don't suppose this girl—" began Stokey.

"No. She hasn't got a thing to do with it! Now go back up and warn Gregory against strange ships and boats."

Stokey looked as though he were about to push his theory further, but he caught a certain glint in his chief's eyes and silently swung himself back to the deck.

Once again the stage was lowered toward the water, and in spite of himself, the words "Death at Twenty Fathoms!" sent a chill racing down Hawk's back. The last thing he saw before the waves buried his glinting headgear were the words and, above them, the anxious face of Vick Stanton as she watched him out of sight.

Sunlight shot through the blue water and the waves made the stabbing rays flicker weirdly through the undersea twilight. Bubbles were rushing upward from the helmet in a silver trail, to burst on the surface in farewell to those watching from the deck. The sound of escaping air mingled with the dull throb of the compressor motor and the crackle of the telephone. Hawk gave an air valve a half turn and felt the suit puff away from him as it filled. He let go one of the platform braces, placed his hand in the region of his heart and surprised himself by feeling the beat of it through a layer of wool, two thicknesses of twill and a layer of rubber. Something seemed to choke him, and he moved his head away from the corselet, only to realize that the pressure was from within and not from without.

"You're yellow," he muttered to himself. "You've got a yellow streak a yard wide up and down your spine." Then he looked out and saw a striped small fish which resembled a convict. "Hello," Hawk greeted, feeling somewhat silly for saying it. "How is it downstairs? Chilly, huh?"

The fish's mouth opened and closed, opened and closed.

"O, yourself!" Hawk grinned, feeling better for his nonsense. The blue water gradually changed to indigo, until the

15

electric lamp Hawk carried threw out the only noticeable light. Deepwater denizens swam up and regarded the strange, round-headed being on the stage, and then went off to tell their neighbors about it. A barnacled shark saw the light and headed for it, blinking and rolling from side to side in anticipation. Hawk felt of the knife in his belt and turned his powerful light until it caught the cruel glint of the sea beast's eyes. The shark swerved away, came back to stare, and then shot upward out of sight.

"You're yellow, too," Hawk said. He felt the platform come to rest against the bottom, and pressed his chin against the buzzer plate in his helmet. "Hello, Sleepy! I'm down!"

"Twenty fathom," came back to him. "Twenty fathom, and everything okay."

"Death at Twenty Fathoms," said Hawk to himself. And then into the phone: "It's black as coal down here. Better tighten up on the lifeline."

The lamp threw its blurry square of light on a waving forest of graceful shrubs which danced silently and slowly in the current, and Hawk leaned forward and placed a foot on the white sand floor of the Windward Passage. Above, he could see an occasional shaft of light filtering through and a dark blob which was the hull of the *Stingaree*. Ahead, he caught the glint of the iron anchor chain from the ship. He was in a familiar world, doing a familiar job, but there was a thickness in his throat, and a bristly feeling up and down his spine which ordered him, for the first time in his tempestuous career, to go slow.

CHAPTER THREE

The Dead Ship's Grave

FIFTEEN minutes of plodding against the soft resistance of water brought Hawk to a clearing in the forest of the sea, and he stood motionless for many seconds beneath the fronds of a dancing fern and studied what met his gaze. Excitement raced in his blood.

There, within fifty feet of him, lay the grotesque, bare ribs of a sailing vessel, reaching forlornly up to the light of the world it had left centuries before. There was something pitiful about the timbers, though there remained little more than a skeleton of the Spanish ship which had once been counted as the greatest in the mighty gold fleet.

Slightly dazed with the thrill of discovery, Hawk looked to his lines, adjusted his equilibrium valve, and then approached the ship. Under him was a hard surface of coral, pitted here and there with patches of yielding sand. His lead shoe struck something harder than coral and he stopped and turned the light down toward his feet.

He saw a brass cannon, dull and eaten by erosion; but even now, after centuries of immersion, a remnant of a coat of arms was still visible. To lift the gun in the world of light and air would have been impossible, but Hawk stooped now and, without seeming effort, turned the cannon on its side and knelt close to the brass. Letters were missing from the inscription below the shield, but Hawk was able to make out several letters which, when pieced and supplemented, spelled out *Ciudad de Oro*.

This, then, was the ship he had come to find, and somewhere near him lay gold to the amount of two million dollars. But Hawk was not thinking of the money just then. There was something about the pitiful skeleton which made him kneel motionless at her side, thinking about the gallant men who had trod her decks, of their hopes and dreams, their colorful swagger. Somewhere in the after part of those bones, toasts had been drunk to a long-dead king. Beautiful ladies had waited for the ship which had never returned, and had mourned the men whose lifeless bodies had lain here in the sea.

Hawk could see her now as she had been then. He could see the proud flag whipping above the white, emblazoned sails. He could fancy the glint of the sun on brass, and see the bone in the teeth of the galleon as it beat up through the Windward Passage, bound for Spain. He could almost hear the sickening crunch of her bows as they had struck the coral of a treacherous reef. He could see her drifting away while men tried to abandon her. And Hawk well knew the sound of a dying ship; the moaning and screeching of escaping air as the precious cargo turned traitor and brought the ship down to its grave.

Hawk shook himself, and with an effort brought his thoughts back to the present.

He got to his feet and walked up to the side of the ship, playing his lamp over the surviving cross ribs. Carefully he examined the position of the beams and was finally able to determine the position of the bow. Then he walked aft, cautious lest he plunge off into a hole, and paced the distance. Noting it, Hawk grasped a timber and sought the air valve with his other hand. The suit filled and puffed out. Gradually he felt the weight lessen against his feet until he was almost floating in watery space.

With a spring that carried him high in spite of the slow motion imposed upon him, he was able to snatch at the end of the beam and look down into the remains of the hull. Carefully separating his lines from fouling timber, he went over the side and drifted down into the blackness.

His feet touched hard metal objects, which proved to be cannons, bolts, pike heads, cutlass handles, chest locks, grappling hooks—in short, anything made of copper and brass which had survived its wood and iron mates. Stumbling and lurching, Hawk walked slowly aft and played his light about him until he saw that he stood where colorful quarters had once housed the chivalry of two worlds.

Confident, his excitement mounting with each passing instant, Hawk moved chunks of metal from his path and watched expectantly for the glint of gold bars or brass chests. But he was doomed to temporary disappointment by the discovery of gaping holes in the cross ribs, which hinted that the three tons or so of gold had long ago slipped through to the sandy floor.

Hawk stopped and scowled at the offending openings, then turned to make his way up over the side once more. He let himself down and noticed, for the first time, that he was dizzy and shaking—too long below, and deadly nitrogen was ready to bubble in his blood.

He shoved his chin against the buzzer plate. "Haul the lifeline tight and note its direction and length. I'm coming up."

"It's about time!" exclaimed the voice on the other end. "I've been listening to you mumble and grumble and swear and exclaim until I'm all wore out! Did you find the stuff?"

"No," breathed Hawk. "No, I didn't find it." It was hard to realize that another world—one of ambition and greed—existed. It was quiet here. Quiet and peaceful, and wondrously beautiful. The forest under the sea . . .

"Hell!" Hawk snapped to himself. "I must be out on my feet!"

CHAPTER FOUR

Silent Death

THE next morning, Stokey climbed into his outfit with much jerking and grumbling. He shot a glance at Hawk, who was seated on a hatch cover beside the compressor. "That *must* be great stuff down there to make *you* lose your head over it. You haven't done that since you were a kid. You ought to know better!"

He grumbled under his breath while he strapped sixteen pounds of shoe on his right foot, "You ought to be in a nut house someplace! Mooning around at twenty fathoms and turning on all the air you've got and having to stay in the pressure chamber for three hours after we drag you up! You won't catch anything happening to *me*!"

Hawk grinned tolerantly, taking his drubbing as a matter of course. After all, it had been silly to forget to shut off his air after he'd made buoyancy serve its purpose. But then, what was a little palsy to a diver?

Vick looked on from afar, smiling in appreciation, and when the stage took Stokey down to the level of the water, she came close to Hawk.

"I'll bet that sign down there gives him the jitters, Hawk."

"Him?" Hawk said. "Give *him* the jitters? Say, that boy hasn't got a nerve in his body! One time we were bringing up a war cargo at thirty feet and I got my lines fouled in some cables, and Stokey came down and dragged me out feet first. He had to cut off his lines to get to me, and we were four hours bringing him around."

"With all the jobs you've done, Hawk, why don't you retire?" Vick sat down beside him and clasped her hands around the knee of her sailor pants. "You must have enough money."

"Oh," snorted Hawk, "money! It's not that—it's the kick you get out of it. It's all so ... so ... well, down there!" He broke off, amused by his lack of adequate words. "You know what I mean. It's rather grand."

Vick nodded and rocked back and forth, gazing out across the water. "I know. It gets you. By the way, how deep can you see in that water?"

"Oh, about thirty feet. After that depth, things are pretty indistinct."

The man on the phone interrupted them. "Stokey says he's down beside the *Ciudad de Oro*. He wants to know which side you saw those holes on."

"Tell him," Hawk said, "that her bow is pointing north, and he ought to dig around on the port side."

The operator relayed the message and then, for the next fifteen minutes, the only noise on the forward deck of the *Stingaree* was the throb of the compressor motor sending its life-sustaining air to Stokey down in the murky depths a hundred and twenty feet below.

Finally Hawk unlimbered himself and stretched. "Ask him if he's found anything besides cannons."

"Okay," said the operator. "Hello, Stokey! *Hello!* Hey! Wake

22

up!" The sailor turned to Hawk, his face strained. "Must be something wrong with the phone line. He doesn't answer."

Unperturbed, Hawk walked over to the rail and gave the lifeline a tug, then held it loosely, waiting for the answering jerk. His mouth tightened and a worrying light showed in his eyes as he pulled the line again. Still no answer.

Just then the buzzer began to rasp out a steady note, and the operator snapped into the phone, "All right! All right! I got it. What is it?" The sailor jumped to his feet and tore the phones away from his head. "I just heard a mumble!" he shouted. "Just a mumble, and something about death! Good Lord! Pull him in!"

With both feet braced against the rail and his hands clenched over the lines, Hawk was bringing Stokey back up.

CHAPTER FIVE

"It Couldn't Happen!"

W HEN the inert form of Stokey Watts was at last brought up to the deck of the ship, Hawk knelt beside him and with shaking fingers stripped the helmet and corselet from the nerveless head. Then, his face clouded with horror, his mouth twitching at the corners, Hawk stared. For Stokey Watts was dead, and his watery eyes were fixed and glassy as they looked up into the sky they would never again see, the damp hair curled down over his forehead.

Vick stifled a cry, her hand across her mouth.

Death was not new to Hawk, but Stokey had been his friend, and now— Hawk ripped away the remaining equipment and sought with shaking fingers for some clue on the dead body. He searched again and again, then looked up at the stricken face of Captain Gregory.

"It's not suffocation, and there isn't a scratch on him, Greg. He had plenty of air—" Hawk's voice went on, toneless, uncomprehending. "There's no reason! I say, there's no reason for him to die like that, Greg!" He covered the face with a tarpaulin and then stood up. "That's what the words said, Greg. 'Death at Twenty Fathoms.' And it was Stokey that got it. Stokey!"

It was not until then that a slip of paper in a rubber envelope attracted attention, although the note had been lashed to Stokey's lifeline and must have passed through Hawk's hands as he pulled in. The phone operator saw it, untied it from the line and handed it to Hawk.

Without knowing what he did, Hawk opened the envelope and took out the note. It was not until he had read a dozen words of the message that he realized what he read.

"Where did this thing come from?" he snapped.

"It was tied to his lifeline," said the operator.

"Tied to his lifeline!" Hawk was incredulous. "But how could anything— Look, Greg! It says:

> Nice, isn't it? Want that to happen to you? He wasn't touched. He didn't know what was wrong. He just knew pain, and then death. You have one alternative, Hawk Ridley, and that is to follow instructions. Otherwise the *Stingaree* will share the fate of the *Ciudad de Oro*. We'd take vast pleasure in blowing you to kingdom come. Tie your charts to a buoy secured to the wreck, and then go back to New York. If anything happens to the charts, or if you make any further attempt to recover the gold, your number is up. Do you get it straight?

"Well, for heaven's sake! The thing isn't even signed!"

"Good Lord!" exclaimed Gregory. "How in the name of the devil could anyone tie that to the middle of a lifeline? And what could happen to kill a diver that way? There's something phony about this, Hawk. I said so from the first, and I still say so."

Hawk thrust the letter into the breast pocket of his jeans

and then turned to look down at the covered body of Stokey Watts.

"Have the men break out my diving equipment, Greg, and get me some tools. I'm going to bury Stokey in his element."

"But you're sick!" cried Vick. "You're sick! You can't do that!" Her eyes were distended with horror. "Supposing . . . supposing that thing that got him! Oh, Hawk, please don't go down there!"

"He'd have done as much for me," Hawk said dully. "I'll dig his grave in the sand and mark it with a coral cross. It's the least I can do."

They replaced Stokey's diving suit and silently fitted the helmet over the round, wind-beaten head for the last time, and when Hawk had dressed, they pulled up the platform and laid Stokey and a small pile of tools upon it.

Hawk's helmet disappeared beneath the blue water, and from the deck, Vick saw that his eyes were dull and unseeing as they looked up toward the sky through the plate-glass window.

Tense minutes flicked by, while the phone operator, half afraid lest silence greet him at any moment, talked incessantly into the mouthpiece. Vick listened to the drone of the man's voice and then walked slowly to his seat beside a switchboard.

"Give me that, please," she said. And with no more than a startled glance in her direction, the man surrendered the instrument to her.

Occasionally she could hear the clink of metal striking rock twenty fathoms down, and she listened, white and drawn, fearful lest the sounds stop. Then she relaxed, and she heard softly spoken words against the background of gurgling water.

From a hundred and twenty feet under the sea, from the realm of white sand and trees dancing weirdly upon a white sand floor, came the ritual for the burial of the dead at sea.

"We therefore commit his body to the deep, looking for the general resurrection in the last day, and the life of the world to come, through our Lord Jesus Christ; at whose second coming in glorious majesty to judge the world, the sea shall give up her dead; and the corruptible bodies of those who sleep in Him shall be changed, and made unto His glorious body, according to the mighty working whereby He is able to subdue all things unto Himself."

There was a pause, a silence broken only by the rush of air through water and then, "So long, Stokey!"

Perhaps it was the simplicity of the service or the revelation that Hawk Ridley—he of the lean, reckless face and youthful swagger—was capable of such depth of feeling, but Vick Stanton cried, unashamed and openly, upon the deck of the *Stingaree*, while the telephone slipped unheeded to the steel plates, to be retrieved by the awed sailor who sat at the switchboard.

"It couldn't have happened!" Vick cried. "It couldn't have happened! Why, oh, *why* did they have to do it? All the gold on the floor of the sea couldn't pay for the death of Stokey!"

CHAPTER SIX

The Voice of Night

TROPICAL rain had begun to fall at supper time, and when the sun had dropped over the horizon to leave the world in darkness, water ran in torrents along the scuppers and crashed against the steel plates of the decks.

Hawk, heedless of the fact that he was clad only in thin dungarees and that the water had long ago soaked him through, sat in solitary vigil near the compressors and stared straight ahead without seeing the rain. For an hour he had remained motionless, mulling over the events of the day and pondering a course of action that might reasonably assure him of victory.

He didn't know what strange thing he faced, and he could not explain the cause of the day's disaster. He knew that Chuck Mercer, of Ocean Salvage, was someway involved, but just how anyone could so strike a salvage ship without showing themselves even for the briefest instant was the problem. He was reasonably sure that Vick Stanton had little to do with it, even though she might be in Mercer's pay.

And then his thoughts were interrupted by the pounding of a diesel engine from the side of the *Stingaree*. Motionless, he listened, his thoughts a whirlpool. It might be a Haitian boat out to contest the *Stingaree*'s right to salvage off the island coast. Again it might be . . .

A voice floated to him through the rain-drenched darkness.

"Go away, I tell you! Go away! They're fully armed, and you wouldn't stand a chance. They have machine guns, understand? Machine guns and depth bombs are waiting for you. Yes, you were seen yesterday, so go! It's the only way you can save yourself."

Hawk stiffened and felt his heart beating in his throat. The person who spoke was Vick Stanton!

"One side!" rasped a voice Hawk failed to recognize. "We'll clear them up here and now. This is our game, not theirs."

Hawk's hand went to his belt, where a Colt .45 nestled coldly inside his waistband. He stood up, balancing himself against the pitch of the anchored ship, and tried to locate the direction of the voices. Then, as cool and deliberate as a duelist, he strode across the slippery steel, his automatic tight in his fingers.

Dark shadows loomed ahead, and the pounding of the engine grew louder. Hawk stopped and drew in his breath.

"Come aboard, gentlemen, come aboard!" he snapped. "I believe we have a little score to settle."

A tension so vivid that it was tangible struck silence to the ship. Then a hoarse tumble of words came:

"It's Ridley! Sweep him down!"

"But the girl!"

"The devil with the girl! Fire!"

Hawk dropped to the deck as though struck and an instant later the sledgehammer blows of a stuttering machine gun crashed out just over his head. Cadmium flame streaked away from the red ball of fire at the gun's muzzle, and the crack of lead on steel drowned the night in savage, imperious tumult.

Hawk leveled the .45 and sighted the caldron of powder flame before him to send a well-placed shot above the gun. A scream, dying as a body arched into the sea, came from the side of the *Stingaree,* and Hawk fired again. For an instant there was silence, save for the crash of water. Then a bellow of rage blasted down from the bridge.

"One side, Hawk," roared Captain Gregory. "I've got a party fixed for those birds!"

The icy white streak of a searchlight leaped down from the superstructure and threw the entire well deck into a brilliance rivaling day. An instant later, pistols and rifles began to hammer through the light. . . .

Before him Hawk saw two masts and a round steel bulk which jutted up beyond the ship's rail, and the surface was studded with swiftly moving men. The bulk seemed to split apart and, an instant later, light-blinded men leaped down to the deck of the salvage ship—a boarding party fully as determined as any pirate horde had been three hundred years before in the same waters. Bodies crumpled under the fire from above, but the invaders were not stayed.

Hawk rolled away from his exposed position into the protection of a hatchway and from there began to snipe away with all the harsh relentlessness born with the death of Stokey.

Men of the *Stingaree* were now sweeping down from the superstructure, to stay the rush before the attackers could barricade themselves on the ship. Hawk caught a blurred

31

glimpse of Vick Stanton as she ran back into the shelter of a passageway, and even in this taut moment of battle, he wondered what possible connection she could have with the attack.

Two *Stingaree* sailors came up abreast Hawk. He jumped to his feet, threw up his arm in the time-honored signal of charge, and swept straight at the thickest of the boarding party. Voices mingled with the clatter of hammering guns and now and then a high-pitched scream told of a bullet taking its toll.

A fight-maddened brute caught Hawk with a mighty hand. Hawk saw a timely glint of a belaying pin as it swept down toward his skull, and twisted away. There came the crunch of brass striking his shoulder and then, just as the blow went home, he fired straight into the face of his assailant, blotting out the bared teeth and narrowed dark eyes.

As the body sagged away from him, Hawk saw Gregory wading in, furious.

There were perhaps fifteen in the boarding party, most of them black and stripped to the waist, the rain pelting against their bare skin. In the glow of the searchlight, their teeth glittered hard and white, and the knives, revolvers and belaying pins threw back a savage fanfare of brilliance.

Hawk fended blows as he sought to discover the leader, but his height made him a target for the center of the rush and he was unable to catch more than an occasional view of the entire melee. All he could see was flailing arms and weaving legs, and his own fists were valiantly battering down any who came within reach.

He felt arms encircle him from behind, but before he could twist about, the grip tightened and he was borne aloft with incredible rapidity and flung a dozen feet along the slippery plates. He brought up against a bitt and scrambled to his feet, but while he was still crouched, a second bulk crashed into him and threw his head down between the iron blocks. A fist caught him on the temple, and the blow was repeated before Hawk managed to free his arms and reach up to drag his attacker down.

The fellow howled under the force of the rib-cracking grip and kicked up with a knee in an attempt to catch Hawk in the groin. Teeth sank into Hawk's shoulder and he brought up a hand to crash the man's skull into the iron bitt. This time the invader went limp. Hawk managed to crawl from under in time to meet a concentrated rush of men.

By now the fight had spread out and the invaders had succeeded in penetrating through to the limits of the searchlight. Shots from passageways and from behind ventilators were beginning to take their toll of the *Stingaree*'s men, and with a quick glance about him, Hawk made a break for the shadows.

He found Gregory crouched behind a locker, automatic in hand.

"They're all through the ship!" Gregory snorted. "We'll play hell clearing them out tonight. What'll we do?"

"Hunt them down!" snapped Hawk. "They're here to wreck us and the equipment, and perhaps to find the charts of the wreck."

"Who are they?"

"How should I know? They came over the side from a boat of some sort. I thought they were Haitians at first, but they all speak English. It's some of Mercer's work. Get that devil behind that ventilator."

The captain carefully sighted the crouching shadow which was silhouetted against the lighted deck, and the man pitched forward and sprawled lifeless, the rain seeming to beat him down and hold him where he fell.

"Come aft," Hawk ordered. "We'll pick them, somehow."

Together they slipped toward the stern, taking advantage of whatever cover offered itself, until they were under the bridge and could make their way with reasonable safety. Hawk found an enemy hovering in a passageway, but before he could do more than send a parting shot, the man disappeared up a ladder. Hawk lowered his smoking .45.

"Collect some of the crew together and make a search. Be quick! Anything might happen! I'm going above to my cabin."

"Why?" asked Gregory.

"Because I think I have a caller. It's impolite to keep people waiting, you know." Hawk gave the captain a crooked grin and swung himself up a hatchway.

For some seconds, he crouched outside his cabin listening. From below came the sound of an occasional shot and the throb of the diesel engine, and now and then a hushed voice penetrated the slither of rain. He gripped his Colt automatic and cautiously thrust in the door, stepping aside, ready to shoot.

"Come out!" he ordered.

Nothing moved in the room. Hawk, standing in the faint blue light of a passageway lamp, spoke again.

"Come out! You won't find anything!"

It was taking a chance to step through the door, for the room was in darkness and the passageway would silhouette whoever tried to enter, but Hawk catapulted himself inside the room and dropped, with the same light motion, to the floor. Flame spat at the place where he had passed the light, and then, aside from hoarse breathing, silence reigned again.

"Drop the gun!" snapped Hawk. "I can see you against the port."

Something crashed against a chair as the intruder leaped away from the supposed light, and Hawk snapped a shot in the direction of the sound. The slug cracked twice into steel before it whined out into the passageway, but from the interloper came no sound.

Cautiously, Hawk raised himself up until he could reach the light switch beside the door, and then, gun held ready, he flipped the button on, switched it off, and dived away just as his visitor fired. The one glance Hawk had taken around the room had told him but little. He knew that the intruder was small and dressed in black, and that there was something vaguely familiar about the man's attitude. For fear that his shots would ricochet to his own disadvantage, Hawk crept silently forward, groping with outstretched hands for the legs of his opponent.

Seconds flicked by before Hawk encountered a leg. Then he snatched back with all his strength and brought a body crashing upon him. Hands reached for Hawk's throat and a gun butt cracked into the floor before he succeeded in rolling over on top of the squirming body. The elation of victory surged up in Hawk as he felt his fists smash the face of the man he held down. Then a fleeting instant turned the tables and the cabin flooded with light.

Hawk tried to leap away from danger, but he was too late. Something crashed into his head. He felt the cabin spin about him, and then, fighting to stay conscious, he slipped to the floor and was engulfed in blackness.

CHAPTER SEVEN

No Quarter

W HEN Hawk came to, he stared up at the kneeling Gregory and tried to raise himself up on an elbow. He sank back with a twisted grin. "I guess they nailed me all right," he said.

"Yes," replied the captain. "They nailed you—and got the charts."

Hawk shot a tense hand under his shirt, to bring it forth empty. "Good Lord! Did they get away?" He managed, this time, to sit up. "What are we going to do, Greg?"

Gregory gave him a hand into a chair and then stood.

"Nothing we can do, Hawk. They'll have some way of disposing of us, now they've got what they want. You should have destroyed those charts after you located the spot and position."

Hawk passed a shaking hand over his face, and then noticed that Vick was in the room. He looked at her for several seconds before he spoke.

"I suppose you've got an answer for all this. Who slugged me?"

"I don't know," said Vick. "My only advice is that you weigh anchor and get away."

"Leave the spot to Mercer?" Hawk stood up, tense and angry. "Well, I'm going down and bring up the stuff, my lady.

I'm not clearing out for an outfit like Ocean Salvage. We can pick them off in daylight, Greg. They can't lower a diver without our seeing them."

"I wouldn't be so sure," Vick murmured.

"What the devil are we up against, anyway?" snapped Hawk. "There's nothing superhuman about those wharf rats. If they put a diver over, they'll have to stand by him, won't they? And if they put a boat near the wreck, Greg can pick them off with rifles, can't he? I'm going to get that stuff if it's my last act on earth!"

"How about Stokey?" demanded Vick. "They got him, didn't they? They got him without ever putting a boat over. And they'll get you." She crossed to Hawk's side and laid a hand on his arm. "Don't be a fool, Hawk! Let them have it!"

"Sure," snapped Hawk. "Turn yellow! It's the thing to do. We're out a fortune, Greg, and don't forget it. There's only one course, and I'm going to take it. How many men did we lose?"

"Two. They lost six. But they got what they wanted, didn't they?" Gregory started toward the door, then turned. "Maybe we're wrong, Hawk. I think we'd better follow the girl's advice."

"Any day I turn tail and run from Chuck Mercer, you can put me in a straitjacket," Hawk snapped.

"Straitjacket, maybe," said Vick. "But even that is better than a coffin." And she ran blindly toward her cabin.

With the coming of daylight, Hawk stepped out on the superstructure and saw that the sky was unusually clear and the sea was as smooth as a skating rink, without so much as a wind ripple to mar the turquoise surface.

Vick called to him from the wardroom. "Come on. Breakfast is getting cold!"

"No breakfast," Hawk said over his shoulder. "I'm going down in about fifteen minutes. You can't eat and do that."

Nevertheless the girl came out with a cup of coffee and watched Hawk swallow the steaming black liquid. When the coffee was gone, Hawk called to a sailor, "Open the lockers and lay out the stuff!" And when the sailor had begun the task, Hawk turned to Vick.

"You ought to know something about this game by this time," he said. "Will you keep an eye on things while I'm below? You may be in somebody else's pay, but I've a hunch you wouldn't want to see me hurt."

"Taking a lot for granted, aren't you?" smiled Vick. "By the way, you haven't a spare outfit, have you?"

"What are you thinking of doing?"

She looked away, then gave Hawk a crooked smile. "Nothing drastic. If you got tangled up below, I thought perhaps you'd like to have someone standing by. You see—I never told you this before, but I've had my initiation undersea. I liked to look at the flowers and fish down there."

Hawk laughed. "What are you trying to do? String me? Oh, well, I'll tell you. There's a self-contained outfit in the lockers. You can fool with that. You know, one of those that doesn't need any air lines or lifelines. I'd rather have my communication and plenty of air, so I rarely use the thing.

If it will make you feel any better, it's there, ready to use. But—and get this—if anything happens to me down there, don't make any grandstand plays. Understand?"

"Yes—and thanks." Vick stepped back into the wardroom.

Gregory helped Hawk mount the platform and saw to it that all was tight with the helmet and corselet, leaving the front window open until the last.

"I hope you'll be all right, Hawk."

"Sure," was the muffled reply. "I'll be okay. I want you to watch for one thing: if you see any boat come around here, keep it on the move. And when I ask for grappling hooks and nets, send them fast. That's your only job. Get them ready now. Vick is going to keep a weather eye open. It will be light down there this morning. Never saw such a clear sea."

Gregory shut the helmet window and listened to the grinding winch which lowered the stage into the sea. He raised his arm in farewell just before the helmet vanished, and Hawk waved back. Gregory had an odd sensation as he saw the hand alone above the water. It was too like that of a man going down for the third time.

Hawk, before he left the surface, had seen the fatal message scrawled on the ship's side. The message, "Death at Twenty Fathoms," which had been Stokey's last connection with the world of light and air. After that he saw only blue, crystal-clear water about him through which fish darted.

A barracuda eyed the diver hungrily and swam so close that Hawk could see the many rows of pointed teeth set in a jaw which ran a quarter of the length of the five-foot fish. But the barracuda thought better of it and went on his way.

The white sand bottom was amazingly clear, though visibility was at no time greater than thirty feet in any horizontal direction. Before, it had been necessary to use the lamp, but now the sea-filtered sunlight was sufficient, and Hawk stepped away from the stage and leaned into the slight current. In a surprisingly short space of time he stood on the edge of the clearing where the *Ciudad de Oro* had lain for centuries. But now he found no time to speculate on the death of the old ship. Dread tugged at him and bade him hurry, and he lost no time in rounding the stern to inspect the sand that must hold the chests of gold.

Then he saw that Stokey had done his work well before he had met his mysterious death. A chest, made of teak and bound with brass, stood upended in the sand, overshadowed by the naked ribs of the galleon, and in the side of the box, with its handle pointed toward the surface, was the weighted pick Stokey had used.

Hawk involuntarily turned and looked back toward the spot where Stokey lay beneath a coral cross, and then, squaring his shoulders, he stepped up beside the chest and pushed it over on its side. Stokey's pick fell slowly to the sand.

It was the work of a second to force the lid of the box, and then Hawk knelt beside it, staring down into a mass of heavy bricks. Gold bullion, greenish under the blue light, was there. Thousands of dollars in gold. But Hawk didn't pause to inspect it closer. A sensation of imminent danger made him pick up his tools and begin work on the pit beside the chest.

It was hard digging, for the water slowed all motion, and the sand, when brought up on the shovel, was half washed away before it could be deposited on the side of the hole. The cavity tended to cave every few minutes, and Hawk was finally forced to enlarge it.

He stopped for an instant and listened, thinking that he heard the sounds of propellers above him. Pressing the buzzer plate with his chin, he called the *Stingaree*. "Anything in sight?"

"No, not a thing," said the operator.

"Thought I heard a prop beat down here."

"Probably the compressor motor. It's missing once in a while."

Vaguely dissatisfied, Hawk resumed his work, and then the feel of his pick striking solidity made him forget for the moment. Eagerly, he dragged a second chest to light and broke its lock. More gold bullion. He quickly estimated that there must be six more chests, and hastily returned to his digging.

One by one he brought them forth, until eight brass-bound teak boxes stood in a disorderly row along the side of the *Ciudad de Oro*. Exertion had caused his head to spin, and when he stood erect, everything turned black. He staggered, caught hold of a beam for support, and then breathed deeply until the world was right again.

As he stood resting, he looked back into the hole and saw the black edge of still another chest. Surprised, he set down his lamp and used his pick to loosen the ninth box. He knew that two million in gold bullion already lay unearthed, and he was unable to account for the ninth. He had estimated that each brick in the chests weighed half a quintal—about fifty pounds—and that there were twelve bars to a box. So he knew that he already had the stated amount of gold.

He broke the lock on the ninth chest and threw his light into it, without suspecting the contents. He gasped and placed the window of his helmet close to the box, lowering his light. There, where he could touch them and pick them up by the handful, lay a green blue caldron of emeralds. He placed his hands on the sides of the chest and stared, hypnotized, for the gems were beautiful and brilliant. He picked some of them up, fondling them, and saw that the greater part were large square stones about as flawless as emeralds can be.

This, then, was the reason Ocean Salvage had wanted the charts. This was why Mercer had stopped at nothing in getting them. He must have known about these emeralds. Compared with the ninth chest, the eight boxes were nothing.

Hawk called the ship, his voice trembling. "Get those nets down to me! Hurry! Snap into it!"

"Coming right down with them," replied the operator. "The captain has them all laid out, ready to go."

Turning to look once more at the precious stones, Hawk stopped suddenly and listened. Pounding against the shell of his helmet came the vibrations of a driving propeller. It was unmistakable this time.

"Anything on the surface?" Hawk snapped into the mouthpiece. "Do you sight any ship? Are any props turning up there?"

"No," came the puzzled answer. "We don't see a thing."

"Well, look sharp, and get those nets down quick!" Hawk

walked a short distance away from the *Ciudad de Oro* and looked up.

A dark blot on the surface was recognizable as the hull of the *Stingaree,* and Hawk watched for the bubbles which would herald the coming of the nets. Then a churn of bubbles and a hurtling shadow far to the north of the ship caught Hawk's attention. He stared, wondering what type of fish it could be. And then—too late—he understood.

"Torpedo!" he yelled into the phone. "Torpedo! A torpedo is coming from the north!"

A shrill babble of sound came back to him through the earphones, and Hawk threw himself flat against the white sand in expectancy of the concussion. He hitched himself under the protection of a coral ledge and looked up again, just in time to see the vicious shape crash into the side of the *Stingaree.*

Concussion smashed Hawk into the sand. When he was able to stagger to his feet, he felt water sloshing inside his helmet. Panic gripped him. Feverishly he felt of the outside of the copper shell which enclosed his head and then knew that the water must have been driven in only by the force of the explosion. A new danger now assailed him, for he saw the hull of the *Stingaree* list to the port, and bubbles told him that the ship was sinking. However, he could still hear the drumming of the compressor motor. Until the ship sank, he would have air.

Then he felt an agonizing twist in the region of his heart as he realized that Vick Stanton might be dead. He didn't ask himself why he thought about her—he only knew that a sudden emptiness had come inside him. He felt helpless, and then, as he realized the difficulty that would come of his lack of air, he knew that he was trapped.

The compressor motor sputtered on, but still air gurgled out of the helmet to send silver globes up to the surface. Hawk leaned back against the current and watched the hull of his ship for endless, fearful minutes. As soon as the compressors went under, there would be no more air, and he could not hope to live more than a few minutes with closed valves. It was possible that they would get a boat over the side. If they did, there would be a little hope.

His attention was suddenly distracted by the appearance of a vague shape on the far side of the *Ciudad de Oro*. Hawk turned to face it squarely. He recognized it, finally, as a diver. The outfit was without hose or line, and hope began to throb through Hawk as he realized that it might be Vick. It was possible that she had had time to don the self-contained suit. She would get him out of this mess if she could.

A hiss above was followed by a second explosion and the *Stingaree* bow went out of Hawk's sight. He saw the stern slide down almost perpendicular, amid exploding air bubbles and the shudders of the dying ship.

A gurgle sounded through the hose line and he reached up to shut off his air valve. The *Stingaree* was finished, and the air compressors had at last reached the level of the water. Working quickly, Hawk unscrewed his hose. And then, after making sure that no one in a boat had hold of the lifeline, he disconnected it.

The second diver was coming closer now and stopped in

the shadow of the *Ciudad de Oro* to stare at the chests. Hawk lunged forward, feeling the tug of water currents caused by the sinking ship. He was anxious to make Vick understand that she must throw off her weights and rocket to the surface. He had already filled his suit to the limit with air, and the increased buoyancy made walking difficult.

In back of him the *Stingaree* was settling to the bottom, still disgorging silvery air. Gear was tangled on the slanting deck, and the chunks of wood about her were shooting to the surface with unbelievable force as they wrested themselves free and deserted. She was here now, dead beside the ship she had come to rob, and as though the better to view her new mate, the *Ciudad de Oro* had shifted a few degrees under the impact of crosscurrents and explosions.

Hawk raised his arm to wave at the diver in the self-contained suit and continued on toward the chests. But the other looked up and failed to return the greeting. Instead, a knife appeared from the weighted belt, catching the blue rays of light that filtered down from the surface.

A little puzzled, though not yet alarmed, Hawk went on till he stood only a few feet away from the other. He was unable to see through the window in the other's helmet, but he was certain that the diver must be Vick.

The chests were between them now, and the other diver stepped up on one. Knife held aloft, he launched himself in a slow-motion dive at Hawk.

The helmets grated together, and Hawk strove to push away the relentless gleam of steel. The other reached out with a savage hand and caught at Hawk's suit, drawing him nearer.

46

Because all action was slow, Hawk was able to sidestep the attack and look into the window of the other's helmet. He frowned, tried to drag the other to him. The knife ripped through two layers of twill and one of rubber, and Hawk heard the rush of escaping air as it went from his suit and bubbled around him like a silvery shroud.

He tried to tear away his weights and escape before the water reached him, but the diver was holding his arms tight, pressing him down against the white sand. Water sloshed up into Hawk's headgear.

Grotesque, like two sea monsters, the divers gripped each other in a savage embrace. The knife fluttered down to the sand, and though his view was marred by seeping water, Hawk saw it and snatched it up. He was gasping for air and could feel the strength ebbing from him, but he managed to hold the knife aloft and bring it down. It came slowly. The other saw it come and tried to step aside, but the steel blade bit into the diver's arm and traveled down, gashing as it went, to admit fatal water.

Hawk was unable to see, and he felt his hold slip as he sagged back against the sand. The hundred and twelve pounds of lead which had been his ballast held him pinned there. With a final slosh his helmet filled with water. . . .

47

CHAPTER EIGHT

Trapped

WITHOUT having the least idea why he was there or where he was, Hawk examined the steel-plated cabin for a clue. A man had just brought him a shot of brandy and then gone out without answering any of the questions shot at him.

Hawk knew that he was somewhere in the Caribbean, probably in the vicinity of the wreck, but he could see nothing but blue sea outside the tiny porthole. For some reason he was being kept intact and a prisoner, but for the life of him he could not figure why. His last recollection had been the sure knowledge that he was drowning, and the next had to do with a pulmotor. After that came a blank, followed by this cabin.

But he had not long to wait, for footsteps came just outside his door. The brass knob wobbled and a key grated in the lock. A short, dark man came in, preceded by a pistol. Hawk sat up on the bunk and glared. It was the man who had been kicked down the gangway in New York, the same man he fought in the darkness of his cabin.

"Hello," Hawk purred. "I suppose you had some good reason for keeping me alive and kicking."

The man smirked and said in a shrill voice, "The old man

had his reasons. Of course, we should have let you soak. You almost drowned Pizer."

"I suppose Pizer is one of your divers, eh? Well, all I can say is that it's a pretty lowdown trick to slit the suit of a man who hasn't any lines." Hawk leaned back and clasped his hands around his right knee. "The way you got me up is a trade secret, I suppose."

"Oh, yes—trade secret." The short one shifted uneasily under Hawk's unwinking eyes. "But I'm not here to gab with you, Ridley. I want to know where you stowed the chest you brought up to the *Stingaree*."

Hawk started, then relaxed before the other had noticed. "Well, Mercer—that's the name, isn't it?—I'll tell you. You're bound and determined to kill me as soon as I give you the information, and—"

Mercer broke in quickly, "Oh, no, nothing of the sort! If you tell us where the chest was stowed, we'll let you off. We might even give you something. The old man said so."

With an easy smile, Hawk drawled, "Yeah? Well, I've different ideas about your brother's code of ethics. Suppose we make a little bargain?"

The beady, dark eyes narrowed. "You ask for bargains? *You!* Why, you fool, if we hadn't picked you up off the bottom—"

"If you hadn't sent Pizer down to finish me, I'd be alive and ashore in Haiti by this time." Hawk's voice was sharp, his whole body taut as he fought an impulse to hand his captor a taste of battle. "We'll make plenty of bargains. That chest"—Hawk grinned inwardly at his own intrigue—"is in a good safe place. You'd never find the strongroom of the *Stingaree* without my help. Call your brother."

Indecision stamped the squat face of Al Mercer, then he slipped out of the door and locked it behind him.

Furious thoughts seethed in Hawk's mind as he saw the door shut and not the least of them dealt with Vick Stanton's whereabouts. It was clear that Ocean Salvage was after a chest which had not been found, and even though Hawk knew less than nothing about the disposition of the box, he determined to play his cards through to the limit.

Heavy footsteps sounded again and two men entered the cabin, carefully closing and locking the door. One was Al Mercer. The other was unmistakably his brother, Chuck, the head of Ocean Salvage Company.

"Hello, Chuck," said Hawk. "It's a long time since I've had the doubtful pleasure."

"It's no pleasure for me," rasped Mercer. "I thought I'd got rid of you a long time ago. Too damned bad your ship's boats got away from us. I was all for leaving you undersea and to hell with the plate, but little Al here got greedy."

"Good thing I did, too," snapped Al. "I told you that chest had all the set emeralds in it!"

His brother glared at him, then turned to Hawk. "Now listen, Ridley. It's no pleasure to talk to you, I'll tell you that, so make this business short and sweet. Where did you stow the emeralds in the *Stingaree?*"

"What's the matter?" Hawk purred. "Is your friend Pizer afraid to putter around a dead ship? Your outfit's too wise to

51

keep a chicken-livered diver. Did you have a good time with your charts? What did you steal the things for, anyway?"

Chuck's lips curled in a snarl. "To look up the chest position, of course."

"Why," exclaimed Hawk with a grin, "I didn't know you could read, Chuck!"

"Cut the comedy, Ridley, and loosen up about that box!"

"Tell you what I'll do, Chuck. I'll write out the directions the minute you put me on the beach over in Haiti."

"To hell with that!" Chuck said roughly. "You're going to tell me here and now. If you're right, I'll set you loose. If you're wrong—well, it'll be just too bad for Hawk Ridley."

Hawk's voice was weary as he leaned back. "Oh, hell, you might just as well have left me by the *Ciudad de Oro*! You've never kept your word in all your life."

Chuck's face grew livid, and he took a threatening step toward Hawk. Al laid a hand on his arm. "You won't get nothing out of him that way."

"No?" Chuck considered a moment. Then his face lit up; he flung the door open. "Come on in here, you devils," he shouted down the passage.

A patter of bare feet greeted the command, and three huge men came in, their faces expressionless.

"Take him out on deck," Chuck ordered. "Take him out and string him up by the thumbs!" He turned to Hawk. "Perhaps now you'll babble. You will—*or else*!"

The three picked Hawk up as though he were a chip of wood and carried him out to the deck. He offered no resistance,

STORIES from the GOLDEN AGE

☐ Yes, I would like to receive my **FREE CATALOG** featuring all 80 volumes of the *Stories from the Golden Age Collection* and more!

Name

Shipping Address

City   State   ZIP

Telephone   E-mail

Check other genres you are interested in: ☐ SciFi/Fantasy ☐ Western ☐ Mystery

FREE SHIPPING!
NO PURCHASE REQUIRED

6 Books • 8 Stories
Illustrations • Glossaries

6 Audiobooks • 12 CDs
8 Stories • Full color 40-page booklet

Fold on line and tape

IF YOU ENJOYED READING THIS BOOK, GET THE ACTION/ADVENTURE COLLECTION AND SAVE 25%

BOOK SET	**AUDIOBOOK SET**
~~$59.50~~ $45.00	~~$77.50~~ $58.00
ISBN: 978-1-61986-089-6	ISBN: 978-1-61986-090-2

☐ Check here if shipping address is same as billing.

Name

Billing Address

City   State   ZIP

Telephone   E-mail

Credit/Debit Card #: _____

Card ID # (last 3 or 4 digits): _____

Exp Date: _____/_____ Date (month/day/year): _____/_____/_____

Order Total *(CA and FL residents add sales tax)*: _____

To order online, go to: **www.GoldenAgeStories.com** or call toll-free **1-877-8GALAXY** or 1-323-466-7815

BUSINESS REPLY MAIL

FIRST-CLASS MAIL   PERMIT NO. 75738   LOS ANGELES CA

POSTAGE WILL BE PAID BY ADDRESSEE

GALAXY PRESS
7051 HOLLYWOOD BLVD
LOS ANGELES CA 90028-9771

STORIES from the GOLDEN AGE

by L. Ron Hubbard

COLLECT THEM ALL!

7051 Hollywood Blvd., Suite 200 • Hollywood, CA 90028
1-877-8GALAXY or 1-323-466-7815

To sign up online, go to:

www.GoldenAgeStories.com

for he was too occupied with plans to waste energy in useless fighting.

Chuck and Al followed the procession.

"String him up!" Chuck ordered a second time, and then found the necessary halyards himself.

Hawk watched the thin line draw tight about his thumbs, and then followed the arc of the rope as it was thrown over a yard. Two of Chuck's men were already pulling. Hawk looked at them calmly, though he knew the terrific pain that would be his in an instant.

CHAPTER NINE

Crash Dive!

I T was not the condition of the rusty tramp steamer that attracted Hawk's attention, for he had seen thousands of ships like her, and he was not puzzled by the appearance of the Santo Dominican flag which flew at the truck. It was the sight of a steel bulk jutting up beyond the ship's rail which gave him a sudden inspiration. The shape of it was familiar, for the same thing had appeared the night of the attack upon the *Stingaree*.

His toes were just going off the deck when he spoke.

"Listen, Chuck. You win. I've got a proposition to offer you."

"Sure," Chuck said. "I knew you'd see light. You're yellow, Ridley. I knew it all along."

Hawk let the insult pass, for there was more urgent business at hand. "I'll not only tell you where that chest is, I'll go down and bring it out myself. And if you want to let me go free after that, it's your business."

"Now you're talking!" Chuck jerked his thumb at the halyard and his men loosened it and slipped it off Hawk's fingers.

"There," said Hawk, limbering up his arms and rubbing his hands. "I see you've got a tin fish over there at the rail. New addition to your firm, isn't it?"

Chuck said nothing to Hawk, but called up toward the superstructure, where a white head appeared in answer.

"Break out your crew!" Chuck called. "Is everything set aboard the sub?"

"Yes, sir!" said the man on the bridge.

Hawk strolled over to the rail and looked down. Below, half out of the water, was a small submarine. Hawk had seen the type before. In fact, he had aided in the salvaging of a submarine a few years before. The only difference or change he could see in the hull was a built-on compartment forward—undoubtedly a compression chamber. He didn't wonder at Mercer's possessing such a boat, for hundreds of them had been bought by salvage firms, solely for the lead contained in the storage batteries. The recommissioning of a submarine would be a comparatively simple matter.

The discovery of the undersea craft explained many things. Hawk understood now why no ship had been sighted when he heard the beat of a propeller. And he understood how the legend had been written on the side of the *Stingaree.* As for Stokey's death, the submarine had probably hovered over him while a diver on its deck injected poisonous gas into the airline.

Three white men and seventeen natives dropped over the side of the tramp steamer to the deck of the submarine and swarmed down through the conning tower hatch. When they had disappeared, Hawk was ordered down, the muzzle of Chuck Mercer's gun at his back.

"Mind you," Chuck rasped, as he watched Hawk go through the hatch, "no funny business, or you'll wish you'd never been born. A lot of things can happen on a submarine."

"So long," Hawk called. "I'll see you anon!"

When the submarine had cast off from the steamer, Hawk

paused in the conning tower to look around at the glittering instruments, at the brass wheels and voice tubes which studded the narrow walls, but he was allowed no time for observation.

"Get below!" snapped the white-headed man. "Can't you see you're cluttering things up?"

Nevertheless, Hawk paused in his drop down the second hatch to note the various instruments used in the manipulation of the boat. In the hull of the boat, he stood in the center of the passage that ran down the entire length of the craft, and marveled at the economy of space.

He had salvaged submarines, but he had never been to sea in one, and he was not quite ready to put his stamp of approval on the idea. A fairly heavy sea was running and the boat rolled with a logy gait that was disconcerting to one used to the even swing of a ship. A multitude of stuffy smells came to him, the acrid odor of burned oil predominated, and the atmosphere was as damp and clammy as a cellar. Huge drops of water were condensing on the inside of the plates and, as the ship rolled, splattered down without regard to men or equipment.

"Lungs," which were to be utilized in case of sinking, were hung up along a bare space beside the conning tower ladder. Far forward were two diesel engines, and behind them were the electric motors used for submerging.

Hawk marveled at the intricacy of construction and then at the fact that the commander of this boat had natives for a crew. And then he remembered the sinking of the *Stingaree* and his jaw tightened. His interest in the submarine lessened.

From above he heard the command "Fill the tanks!" Several

of the crew elbowed by him on their way to valves. Hawk found a bunk and, by stooping, found that he could sit down upon it. Drops of water fell on him, but he wanted to be out of the way so that he could think.

At the command "Dive!" the motion of the boat changed, as it went down by the nose. Then Hawk knew that they were under the waves. He saw the man at the "diving piano" crouch, working the levers in the conning tower. The only sound, outside of the gurgling water, was the purr of the electric motors driving the undersea craft toward the wrecks of the *Stingaree* and the *Ciudad de Oro*.

One of the white men approached Hawk with the command to follow him and they went down the passageway to a locker where the pieces of a self-contained diving outfit were stowed. In silence Hawk pulled on the suit and laced the legs, fastened the lead shoes and adjusted the corselet.

The white man watched the performance with calculating eyes. "Know how to adjust that airflow?"

"I invented it!" Hawk said dryly.

"You've got two jobs to do, you know," the other said. "You've got to move those chests into the sub before you go after the one in the ship."

Hawk's smile vanished. "What the—" he began angrily, then stopped. "All right with me, but you'll have to change this air tank before I go after the one in the ship."

"That's okay, we've three or four of them. Need any help?"

"No. Say, by the way, isn't there some way you can watch me out of this thing? I might get messed up and need help." Hawk's smile was innocence itself, but he was thinking fast.

"There isn't any way. If you get messed up, that's just too bad. We can see a little way out of the ports in the tower, but it's too dark below today." The man looked back along the ship. "We're going to settle on the bottom in a minute, so be ready."

Hawk listened to the faint scrape of sand against the hull as the boat came to rest on the bottom. Then he watched the men open up the compression chamber on the forward deck. He fastened the lugs on his helmet and shuffled to the bottom of the narrow ladder, where willing hands pushed him up. Then he was alone in a cell-like room, and he heard water begin to rush in upon him. The sensation was a little disturbing, for he had not tested the helmet to his satisfaction. But there was nothing to be done about it, and he felt for the dogs on the outer door to make sure they were movable.

Turning on the small hand lantern hooked in his belt, he watched the water rise up and engulf him, and slowly turned his airflow valve to adjust it with the increasing pressure.

Finally he took the dogs off the watertight door and stepped out into the murk of a hundred and twenty feet below the waves. Before he clambered down the side of the submarine, he turned his light into the chamber. Yes, a compressor valve was handy, in case he wanted to enter without help from below. Satisfied, he stepped off and floated down until his feet struck the sand.

Evidently things had happened too fast to suit the Ocean Salvage men, for they had deserted the nine chests that lay under the side of the *Ciudad de Oro.* All the lids were in place, just as he had left them.

He approached the first gold chest and tried its weight. Then he picked up a tool and slowly dug into the sand until he struck a hard substance—the chest.

Hawk smiled to himself as he laid the box beside the other nine, for the joke was on Chuck Mercer. When the cover was opened, plate, studded with emeralds, gleamed up. It was clear that Chuck Mercer believed Hawk had been at work taking the chests to the surface when he was interrupted. It was a small error on Chuck's part, but it had saved Hawk's life.

Hawk began the work of transporting the chests to the submarine, and he smiled each time he laid a box down beside the rusty hull of the undersea craft. It would have been impossible for one man to lift the seven-hundred-pound chests in the realm of light and air, but the added buoyancy of the water made it comparatively easy work.

A half-hour later saw the tons of gold bullion and a nation's ransom in emeralds stowed inside the compression chamber, ready for transfer into the hull. At first Hawk had contemplated stalling for time on the tenth chest, but now, with only an hour's supply of air remaining in his tank, he changed his plans radically. He kicked the side of the ship to signal that all of the chests were within the cubicle and that the place could be flooded from the inside.

He knew that he would receive little mercy at the hands of Ocean Salvage should he re-enter the submarine, so, with characteristic audacity, he decided to trap the boat on the bottom of the sea. If he could clog ballast vents and freeze the elevators, there was little chance that the craft could be brought to the surface before Hawk wanted her raised. If he could accomplish this, he could come back when the boat was empty of men, undo his work, and do as he saw fit with the submarine and its cargo.

Hawk's salvage work had taught him something of submarine construction. He remembered that in one case the submarine had been low on air pressure and incapable of blowing its tanks. The boat had sunk to the bottom of the sea with all hands, of course, there to remain until divers brought her up with pontoons.

This boat, as Hawk had observed, was amply supplied with artificial lungs which enabled the men to leave the craft on the bottom and rise to the surface without receiving anything more serious than a ducking. And when the boat was overdue, Mercer would undoubtedly come to the scene in time to rescue the crew.

As the submarine is ballasted with sea water, and the tanks are all between the two separate hulls of the ship, Hawk's task was simplicity itself. He had only to stop up the vents that allowed the water to be blown out into the sea, and the craft would be unable to move. And he could fix the elevator fins so that they could not be moved from inside.

In order that the boat could not leave before he completed his task, he made his way to the stern, Stokey's pick clutched in his hand. He ran skilled fingers over the control surfaces until he found the grooves that connected the fins to the hull. The arrangement was similar to that of an airplane, where the horizontal flippers are used in gaining and losing altitude.

With the elevators wedged securely down, each drive of the propellers would tend to thrust the boat's nose down, instead of up.

Hawk dragged on the huge sheets of metal until they almost touched the ocean's floor, hoping as he did so that no one aboard the ship had noticed the corresponding motions of the "diving piano." This done, he thrust Stokey's pick into the opening in such a way that a movement of the fin from the inside would be impossible.

When he had done this, he collected a quantity of sea moss and ooze, and stuffed each and every one of the ballast tank vents. Certainly, he thought with satisfaction, the submarine would have to remain right there until he wanted her to move.

But as he walked away from the trapped undersea craft, he felt no elation in the knowledge that he had outwitted Chuck Mercer. He was far too worried about Vick Stanton. He knew that the girl had had time to don the self-contained suit he had indicated, and if she had done so, thinking that she might be able to help him, she was either dead or in Mercer's hands. Hawk was not quite sure which fate would be the worse.

Behind him came the throb of propellers, and he turned to look back at the dark blob the submarine made on the bottom. They were trying to lift her now, without waiting for Hawk's return. It was nothing to them that they meant to abandon a man to death on the sea floor. A mirthless grin came to Hawk's lips as he saw the nose of the boat bump the sand and then plow forward, bow down. He knew that they would try this for some time before they'd realize that they were trapped. Then they would leave the craft before their air gave out, and the boat and treasure would be Hawk's whenever he cared to return—that is, if he lived to come back.

Ahead was the dead *Stingaree,* a shapeless lump of metal in the twilight. Hawk approached her with mixed feelings. He knew only too well the things men encounter aboard sunken ships, and when one's own men . . . Perhaps he might even find Vick.

He forced himself to go on until he could reach the rail. He pulled himself up, steeled his nerves for a glance about the twisted, shadowy deck. But he saw nothing even faintly resembling dead men.

Making his way amid tangles of cable and hawsers, he came upon a wood hatch cover which had been so securely battened with iron lugs that it had been unable to wrest itself free and shoot to the surface. A small line was close at hand, and he slashed off a hundred-foot length and secured one end to the cover. In a moment he had released the lugs. Like a bird suddenly released from nerve-racking captivity, the wood zoomed upward, its speed incredible.

Hawk held the line which now connected him to the surface in one hand. With the other, he unstrapped his shoes and weights, fastening them to the rope so that he could haul them up after he had reached the top.

He went up the line slowly, taking care not to shoot to the surface too quickly and thereby become a victim of the bends.

Within the hour he was again above the waves, holding fast to the hatch cover.

It was good to be on top once more, able to breathe the

free air. And it was good to know that, with a fair share of luck, he would soon be out of Mercer's reach. The tide set was causing a current that would bring him close to the Haitian shore; close enough for him to swim in.

There in those brown, jagged mountains his men must be, safe.

CHAPTER TEN

Twisted Tables

THE current had been kind to Hawk and the wind had helped to bring the wooden grating in toward the beach below the jagged mountains of Haiti. There he deserted his strange craft and stood looking to the right and left, undecided which direction to go to reach the camp his men must have made. All that remained of his diving suit was the twill covering, and this tended to keep the water against his body, making him cold in spite of the warm breeze from the east. Finally, he saw a pinpoint of light glowing on the side of a hill. He struck out, glad to have a destination.

He turned once and looked back at the sea. Far out on the dark water he saw the glimmer of anchor lights on Chuck Mercer's steamer. Mercer's crew would be picking up the survivors of the submarine by this time, and cursing Hawk Ridley roundly and with fervor. The thought made Hawk grin. He went on.

Then, out of a shrub's cover, came the challenge, "Halt, and advance slow!"

It was Dawson, the first mate. Hawk gave him a thin smile.

"Gone blind?" he said.

"Lord, Hawk! We thought you were dead!" the man cried.

"You pretty near guessed right. Where's Vick?" Hawk shot the question as though it were a bullet.

Dawson stammered and then glanced back at Gregory, who was running up. Obviously the mate wanted the captain to answer the question.

Gregory's boisterous greeting was cut short by Hawk.

"Where's Vick?" he snapped.

"Why... you see . . ." Gregory began, not daring to look Hawk in the eye.

"I see!" snapped Hawk. "You let her go down in that self-contained suit to try to give me a hand. A fine lot of heroes you turned out to be!"

"I knew you'd get sore," said Gregory defensively. "I tried to stop her, but I never dreamed the girl had such courage. She jumped over right where you went down!"

Hawk took a step back toward the beach, then stopped. "If they picked me up, they've got *her*. I'm going back to Mercer's ship for her," he said crisply.

"But what do you want me to do?" Gregory's protest was almost a wail.

"Take whatever boats you've got and wait for me at the spot where the *Stingaree* went down. I'll be there before the night's over." Hawk started toward the beach, but Gregory stopped him with a forceful hand.

"Wait a minute, Hawk!" cried the captain. "You're crazy! What's the idea dashing off after that girl and leaving us in the lurch? If she's aboard Mercer's ship, that's where she wants to be. She's in his pay, anyhow. Have some sense!"

Hawk shook him off. "I happen to be giving the orders here—you seem to forget that. I've got to get a diving suit and rescue that girl."

"Grandstand stuff!" exclaimed Gregory, but Hawk's voice cut in.

"Stand on and off with those boats!" he snapped. "I'll take care of my end of it." And swiftly he went out of the ring of men and back to the water he had so lately escaped.

Three boats were drawn up on the sand. Hawk lost but little time in launching the smallest and picking up the short oars. He was achingly tired, but in his excitement he failed to notice. He had only one thought: he must find Vick Stanton.

A half-hour later found Hawk rowing close to the Ocean Salvage steamer. Lights came across the quiet water in long, shimmering paths. He turned now and then to look at the ship and correct his course. And, with the thrill of approaching danger, his heart beat a little faster with every pull of the sweeps.

Caution was the essence of his approach, for if he was discovered too soon, it would all be over. But he did not expect that his move would be counted upon, and therein lay his advantage.

The bow of the cutter grated against the rusty side, close to a dangling line. Hawk secured his painter and began to climb up hand over hand to the silent deck.

It was dark, but he knew that he would be visible at close quarters, especially when he reached the glittering lights of the deck. Silently he pulled himself up, till he could see the well of the ship, where the halyard of his former torture swayed in the night breeze. He was about to drop down when a movement to the right caught his eye. A sentry stood there, half-asleep. Hawk watched him narrowly. Then he inched along the outside of the rail until he was within three feet of the guard.

His fist doubled, Hawk estimated the length of the swing, and then, without ceremony, sent a blow crashing to the fellow's jaw. With a weary sigh, the sentry slumped down into the shadow of a bitt.

Hawk made his way up a ladder to a passage where cabin doors emitted cracks of light. An occasional snore reached his ears as he crept along, crouching before each keyhole to peer in.

He saw Chuck and Al Mercer sitting over a bottle, discussing some weighty matter in low tones. They seemed angry. Then he discovered the three officers he had left on the submarine, and was glad to know that the artificial lungs had permitted the undersea crew to escape from the trapped boat. Finally, he saw an arm over the side of a bunk and knew that he had found Vick Stanton. He tried the door cautiously and found that it was locked, then he went into a dark cabin and found the key in the door. Armed with this vital bit of brass, he went back to Vick's cabin. The key fitted. He turned it and pushed the door wide.

Vick sat up, blinking at the disheveled apparition in her doorway.

"Vick!" whispered Hawk. "Are you all right? Has anything happened?"

Her whisper was vibrant with emotion. "You're safe, then! Hawk!" Tears brimming in her eyes, she buried her face in the folds of his diving dress.

"Slip on a jacket," Hawk said gently. "Do you know where they keep their diving outfits?"

She nodded, donned a coat, then stepped out into the passageway and silently led him down to the well deck. Lockers stood there, disgorging their contents in a disorderly fashion.

"Be careful, Hawk—they've got guards all around here."

Stepping on top of a chest, Hawk turned out the bulb of the deck light. "I don't think they'll notice. Get into a suit, quick!"

For Hawk it was a simple matter. He had merely to add corselet, helmet, tank and weights. But Vick, shaking with excitement, had a much longer task to perform. Hawk helped her with the buckles and laces.

Then, carrying their thirty-two-pound shoes in their hands, and staggering under the weight of lead and copper, they made their way to the cutter's moorings. Hawk brought the small boat down the rail to the Jacob's ladder.

Just as Vick was going over the side a piercing cry rang out. Hawk turned and stared back through the window of his helmet. A scurrying body left the deck and plunged at him. He struck, and his assailant fell to the steel plates. But the warning had been given, and the entire ship came alive with shouting men.

"Into the boat!" shouted Hawk, forgetting that Vick couldn't hear him. He saw, then, that she was already standing on the thwarts of the bobbing cutter, and he wasted no time in scuttling after her.

Above him the rail was lined with men. Then flame began to lash down into the cutter as shots flew after the escaping pair.

*Then flame began to lash down into the cutter
as shots flew after the escaping pair.*

Vick loosened the painter and pushed away from the side of the steamer, then stumbled back to snatch at an oar. Hawk had already begun to pull the sweeps with all his might, but the suits were heavy and the cutter bobbed sluggishly.

Hawk looked up just in time to see a heavy object hurtle down from above. It was a lead weight, and Hawk groaned as he understood. They were heaving missiles at them in an attempt to sink the boat. He had no more than understood when he felt the cutter lurch, then saw water begin to rush up from the bottom of the craft. Vick had also seen, and they bent as one to strap on their diving shoes. Hawk adjusted his own valve and then gave Vick's a twist. All about them bullets were kicking up small, vicious geysers in the dark water and sending phosphorescent streaks into the depths.

Holding the girl close to him with one hand and gripping a lamp with the other, Hawk plunged over the side and into the refuge of dark water.

CHAPTER ELEVEN

An Eye for an Eye

IT was a strange world of blackness, where trees waved slowly and gently and unsuspected hillsides rose up and fell away with appalling suddenness.

Hawk Ridley and Vick walked side by side, unable to express their fears and hopes, held dumb in the silence of a copper helmet through which came only the faint gurgle of escaping air. The waterproof compass Vick had found in her belt helped them, but Hawk looked beyond the reach of their marine lamp and wondered whether they were walking out into the Caribbean, or approaching the wrecks as he had calculated.

It was hard to gauge distance, for their steps were either long or short in accordance with the bottom, but now and then Hawk saw a plant or rock or hill that looked familiar and took heart.

Then Vick tripped over a metal object and stooped to pick it up. Hawk turned the light on it and nodded. It was a valve wheel that might possibly belong to the dead *Stingaree*.

They made their slow way around great, fantastic ferns where sea beasts might lurk, and walked across white sand clearings decked with weirdly beautiful flowers and coral plants colorful beyond description.

At last Hawk stopped with a sigh of relief: far to their right he had caught the gleam of metal through the black water. He led Vick on until they stood in the triangle formed by the wrecks of the *Ciudad de Oro,* the *Stingaree* and the temporarily helpless submarine.

Hawk went to work immediately and inched himself along the rusty sides of the undersea boat till he had cleared out all the vents he had stopped up. He allowed himself a grin as he pulled the pick out of the horizontal fin joint and worked the elevators up and down to assure himself they were ready for his purpose.

He boosted himself up the steel plates until he stood outside the compression chamber. The watertight door was closed on the outside, as he had left it, and he prayed that the deserting men had been farsighted enough to leave the cell flooded for future salvage.

Gritting his teeth against the possible insweep of water which might batter him against the plates, Hawk swung the door open. All was well within. He helped Vick up beside him then, and together they entered the small room and made sure the watertight door was securely closed.

When the water had fallen away from them and the pressure had lessened, they slipped down the hatchway and into the submarine.

Hawk searched about for switches and clicked on the light. He was thankful to note that the deserting commander had made every provision for retaining the boat's seaworthiness. All was in readiness for the ascent.

Vick started to take off her helmet, but Hawk placed his

copper shell close to hers and shouted, "Don't! The air's bad down here. Help me find the ballast valves!"

It was no easy task, lumbering about in a cumbersome diving suit in those narrow confines, nor was it the simple work of a moment to discover the key valve wheels which would blast compressed air into the ballast tanks and force out the sea water. But, after many efforts, Hawk managed it.

In the control station high in the conning tower, he threw in the switches that started the electric engines, and smiled with satisfaction when he heard them purr into life. He gave the "diving piano" a dubious study, then decided upon several of the metal arms and he pulled them toward him.

Sand rasped against the hull, and the submarine lurched, coming up by the nose. The sound of rushing water filled the control room. The boat was surfacing in good order.

In a few minutes the undersea craft leveled itself out, and Hawk shut off the engines with a sigh of relief. He pushed up the conning hatch and then jerked off his helmet. It was good to breathe deep of the night air.

Vick came up to the bridge and sighed gratefully, tossing her fair hair out of her eyes. By the light from the hatchway, Hawk caught a glimpse of her face and he reached out for her hand. They looked at each other for a long, understanding moment.

The creak of hastily plied oarlocks came close beside the submarine, and in another instant, Gregory came into the light. His voice was taut with excitement.

"There's a steamer close aboard! She's heading to ram you!" he cried.

Hawk spun about and gazed across the water. What he saw was a scene he was not likely ever to forget. Mercer's tramp steamer was charging full steam upon them. Lights blazed from the vessel's bridge, and by the gleam of the jackstaff globe, Hawk could see a fury of water hurling away from the speeding bows.

Mercer's intention was plain. The submarine's usefulness was at end, and even if it sank, Mercer would encounter little difficulty in recovering the treasure at his leisure. It was clear that the steamer was about to ram. And if those knifing bows so much as touched the hull of the undersea craft, it would mean the death of everyone aboard. Too late Hawk realized that the hatchway light had betrayed them.

The captain and his men were already swarming over the conning tower and scurrying down into the boat. The *Stingaree*'s chief engineer was at work on the diesel engines, and Gregory was ready at the helm. Hawk dragged Vick down into the control tower and saw, in one brief glimpse, her horror-stricken eyes as she crouched back out of the way.

An eternity passed before Hawk heard the sullen chug of the starting diesels. To the port came the steamer, some two hundred yards away—so close that the figures on her lighted bridge were plain and the churn of bow water looked like froth.

The submarine's forward movement was agonizingly slow. Gregory was white with anxiety.

"We can't dive!" he shouted at Hawk. "These men don't know the valves! And we're too slow to outmaneuver him."

Hawk nodded grimly and glanced at Vick, sorry that she had heard. She tried to smile at him. Hawk cursed himself for not taking to the cutters, then realized that in those fragile boats they would have had less chance than in the submarine.

From below came the chief engineer's nervous shout: "She's got all she can take!"

A hundred yards now separated the two boats, and though the submarine had made some slight progress forward, the steamer changed its course to intercept her. Searchlights were lancing the water with long, bright fingers.

Through the hatch Hawk could see the white faces of the *Stingaree*'s men as they waited tensely, looking up into the conning tower, relying solely upon the judgment of Hawk and their captain.

Above them loomed the high, sharp prow of the steamer, an executioner's blade, ready to sever the life cord of its victim. For a century-long moment it seemed inevitable that the undersea craft would be rammed and sent to the bottom with all hands. But Gregory, wheelwise from a life on the sea, suddenly gave the helm a terrific spin. With a shudder, the submarine lurched drunkenly, swerved, and came about almost at right angles to her course.

The steamer rushed by on the port side, with barely more than a foot to spare in passing.

"We're safe for a minute!" Gregory yelled. "But those devils will come back, and if they try a second time . . ."

"I know," breathed Hawk. "They'll get us."

Vick was at his elbow, her face raised to his. "Isn't there something you can do to them? Isn't there some way you can sink them?"

"I'm afraid not. Perhaps we'll get away the next time, too."

"There's no need to hold the truth from me, Hawk. I know there isn't a chance. They'll cut us down. It isn't the dying I mind so much, it's the thought that Mercer will win." She pointed down into the hull, where a row of brass-bound chests glinted dully under the electric lights.

Gregory abruptly spun the wheel. "Here they come!"

Hawk stared at the turning steamer. His eyes were dull as he realized the hopelessness of their position. He couldn't bear the thought of Vick's suffering so cruel a death. Protectively he placed his arm about her shoulders and drew her close. She smiled, and he returned the smile wanly, his heart aching.

Once more the steamer came straight on her course. Her bow was outlined by the cold beam of her searchlights which flickered over the submarine's hull. Though she was still a thousand yards away, it was clear that she did not intend to be eluded this time. She was coming with redoubled speed, heralded by a phosphorescent spray which shot up half the height of her bow.

Cold hate came into Hawk's eyes as he watched, and his hand closed so tightly over Vick's shoulder that she winced. Hawk glanced helplessly over the maze of buttons and tubes that decked the inside of the conning tower. Then he stiffened and shot Gregory a significant look.

There beside the "diving piano" were four buttons. They were marked "Torpedo Tubes. Bow 1. Bow 2. Stern 3. Stern 4."

"Greg!" Hawk's voice shook with excitement. "Do you think those things are loaded?"

"Why not?" cried Gregory. "Listen. Topside there's a sight. I saw it when I came down. If you'll go up there and take a bead on the ship, we'll fire it below! Quick! You haven't much time!"

"I'll fire it," said Vick.

"Okay!" Hawk snapped. "Take off that cover, and when I yell 'Fire!' press the button marked Three!" He saw her nod, and then turned to run up to the exposed bridge.

A searchlight was holding the conning tower in its unwavering glare. It was into this that Hawk moved. The range was now but a little more than five hundred yards. Rifle fire would not be long in coming.

He shouted down the hatch to Gregory. "Port ten degrees!"

"Port she is," answered the captain.

When the sub had changed course and was running directly away from the steamer, Hawk placed his eye to the cross-work of wire and rods which made up the torpedo sight. The apparatus was mounted in such a way that when the sight was dead on its target, the submarine was pointed in that direction as well.

He intended to use the stern tubes so that they could launch their torpedo while they were running away from the ship. It was taking a chance to utilize so small a target as the bow of the steamer, but there was no time to angle for a broadside shot. Failure in the attempt would mean death for all hands.

Every few seconds Hawk corrected Gregory's course. The sea was running in long swells, and as each one passed under the submarine it threw the sight away from the charging bow of the steamer. He knew that he must allow for a two-second delay in the execution of the firing order, and he waited tensely till he was certain of a shot.

At a distance of five hundred yards, it was possible that the concussion of the explosion would damage the undersea boat, but Hawk gave no thought to that risk.

It was not until they were running in the trough of the waves that he saw his chance. The cross wires of the sight held to the center of the steamer's charging prow. Hawk gripped the rail convulsively. "Fire!" he shouted, and saw Vick's slim hand crash down on the fatal brass disk.

The submarine shook under the jar of the torpedo leaving its tube. The stern was suddenly alive with the fire of phosphorous as the slim shell clove the water. At a speed of thirty knots, a warhead crammed with high explosive was rushing toward the steamer.

Hawk held his breath. He couldn't see the wake of the missile now. He could only guess—and hope.

A hush of expectancy fell over the submarine. All on board waited for the result.

Suddenly the entire sky seemed to shatter into a vertical band of flame. The submarine shook, and Hawk was knocked back by the force of the air. Debris rained across the water like hail and pounded on the steel plates like machine-gun fire.

Then, as quickly as it had begun, it was all over. Fitful flames were licking up around the doomed hull of the ship. Men went plunging over the steamer's side, into the water.

Unsteadily, Hawk made his way down to Vick's side. "Put about, Greg. We're going back and pick them up."

Reaction struck Vick, and she dropped down into the small seat against the bulkhead. She sat there, her face buried in her hands, weeping silently. Hawk placed his arm about her, and when she looked up he leaned down and kissed her.

"It's all right, Vick," he breathed. "We're all right now."

She nodded silently, trying to manage a smile.

CHAPTER TWELVE

Northward Ho!

IT was later, much later, when all was quiet on board the submarine and the work of rescue was over. Men lounged in the narrow bunks in the hull, tired from the tremendous strain of the night.

Up toward the bow, in the torpedo room, two prisoners sat disconsolately against the bulkhead and glowered at each other. Hastily improvised irons were about their ankles and wrists, and with the added precaution of the guard at the door, it was certain that the doom of the Mercer brothers had been sealed. They would go north, into the hands of the courts. If they managed to be acquitted on the charges of murder, the best they could look forward to would be a lifetime spent behind bars.

Further along the passageway were ten brass-bound, glinting chests which held several fortunes in gold bullion, and a nation's ransom in emeralds.

Aft of these, two diesel engines were pounding along at their best speed, safe in the care of the *Stingaree*'s chief engineer.

In the conning tower, a sailor stood at the wheel and looked down into the binnacle which read *North*. From time to time he looked up through the hatch to the open bridge above, whence came the pleasant murmur of voices.

From the open bridge it was possible to look out across

the water to the east, where the clouds were catching up the rays of the coming sun, relaying their light to the dark ocean, promising a new day.

But neither Vick nor Hawk Ridley was paying much attention to the sea. They stood close together at the rail, finding it enough just to look at one another. Gregory, on the far end of the bridge, glanced at them from time to time with friendly, amused eyes.

The light in the east became so brilliant that it could no longer pass unnoticed, and Vick spoke, her voice hushed by the beauty of the scene.

"It's the most glorious dawn I've ever seen," she said.

Hawk gave the horizon an appreciative glance.

"I don't think I've ever seen a finer one myself. But it might be better, Vick."

She looked at him, puzzled. "What do you *mean*?"

"I might as well tell you now, while we have beauty to temper the hurt. I want to know one thing. Are you married?"

"Why? What makes you think—?"

"You came aboard in a wedding dress. I've been worried ever since you came aboard."

Vick laughed softly. "And if I really am married," she said, "would it make so much difference?"

"You know it would!" Hawk cried, so fervently that Gregory almost dropped his field glasses.

Vick looked out across the water.

"I'm not married, Hawk. I never have been. But I didn't want to tell you until—until all this was straightened out. But I can tell you now. I hope it won't make any difference."

"How could anything make any difference?"

She drew back a little before she spoke.

"On the night you sailed, I was about to be married to Al Mercer, Hawk."

"That runt!" he exclaimed.

"Yes. I couldn't do anything else. I had to—for Dad's sake. Dad, you see, is the financial backer of Ocean Salvage."

"I knew that," Hawk said.

"And Chuck Mercer told Dad that if I didn't consent to marrying his brother, he would expose some of Dad's deals. He said that Dad had gone outside the law in backing a certain ship salvage Chuck had handled. Dad laughed, but Chuck and Al had some clever lawyer prove that they were right—some technical point. I went to another lawyer, but I didn't think it would do any good. They're so slick, Chuck and Al."

She paused for an instant, giving Hawk's tense face a brief, troubled glance before she went on.

"And so, on the night I was supposed to marry Al Mercer, everything was in readiness. All the guests, the minister, Dad—everybody was there. I was dressed, waiting to go downstairs, trying to get up courage for the ordeal. I guess I'd do anything for Dad. And then—well, my lawyer telephoned me and explained that Dad had been right, and that the Mercers had nothing real to go on. I called Dad, but he was upset and afraid of Chuck and Al. He said I had to go through with it. He said it would mean the end of things for both of us if I didn't.

"I waited until he had gone back to the guests, then I ran

away. I went down the back way and out into the street. I had no money, and no place I could go. I didn't even have any clothes but the wedding things I was wearing. Then I remembered that you were sailing. I'd read about it, and I had heard Al say that he had been unable to get some charts you had. And so—well, I knew from your reputation that you were decent, and—well, here I am."

He kissed her.

"You bet you're here!" Hawk said, holding her in strong protective arms. "And you're going to stay right here, too. When we get back to New York—you'll marry me, Vick?"

"Yes," she said.

"And we're going to pave the church steps with emeralds and have the altar made out of gold! How does that suit you?"

"Hawk, I'd marry you in a diving suit and at the bottom of the sea!" And to confirm the statement, she gave him a kiss as rich with promise as the scarlet light of dawn.

Story Preview

Story Preview

NOW that you've just ventured through one of the captivating tales in the Stories from the Golden Age collection by L. Ron Hubbard, turn the page and enjoy a preview of *Sea Fangs*. Join Bob Sherman who, in an attempt to reclaim oil fields stolen from him, secretly hires on as a deckhand aboard the yacht of Herbert Marmion, the man who ruthlessly stole them. When a hurricane sends the yacht to an uncharted island, the entire crew is captured by pirates—including Marmion's beautiful daughter, with whom Bob has fallen in love.

Sea Fangs

SHERMAN had the papers of a master mariner down in his sea bag, but he was not going to unfold his hand just yet. It was not his business if the *Bonito* sprung every rivet in her trim hull. Still, he had shown Stoddard that dropping barometer, had even explained what a hurricane meant down here off the treacherous coast of Venezuela. And Captain Stoddard had told him to finish painting the stack and leave seamanship to someone who understood it.

The caking salt on Sherman's cheeks had long ago begun to eat into his bronze skin, and the spray had found its stinging way down inside the slicker, making his clothes cling to his hard body. But there was something in this fight with the hurricane that avenged all the wrongs the sea had done him in the past three years. In reality, of course, the misdeeds lay at the door of Herbert Marmion and a certain outfit of outlaw smugglers and revolutionists who held sway over their small islands a few miles out from the Gulf of Venezuela. But the sea's brute force, brought to him through the broken ports, was ample challenge to his tremendous strength, and Bob Sherman fought on.

The chief officer, a silky man named Hardesty, came out of

a passageway and tapped Sherman on the shoulder. "You've had it an hour!" he yelled. He motioned two sailors out of the passage and to the wheel.

The two sailors laid trembling, and immediately wet, hands upon that terrible wheel, and looked up at Sherman. He released the wheel as though the action was distasteful to him.

"The stewards," cried the chief officer, "are all in their bunks. Will you go below and lend a hand?"

Sherman nodded assent and stooped to enter the open door. Bracing himself against the sides of the passageway, he worked his way aft. At the top of a companionway he pulled his sou'wester from his hair and whipped the streams of water away from his coat. Then he pulled the oilskin hat over his right eye and dropped to the lower deck.

He found himself in the main salon and paused for a moment to stare around at the havoc the storm had caused. Heavy chairs lay broken on their sides. The grand piano had lost all but one of its legs. Drapes were tangled about mahogany tables, and rugs were snarled bits of color on the water-soaked deck.

Sherman held to a rail for support and stood there with a grim smile on his face. It gave him something like pleasure to see the belongings of the Marmions so drastically ruined. He glanced toward the row of doors which designated the owner's quarters and smiled again. All the Marmions and their friends were within those doors, seasick, stricken with fear. But as he looked one of the doors swung back, and Sherman found himself looking at Marmion's daughter.

She was black-haired and dark-eyed. Her face was drawn

with worry, but when she saw him she smiled and picked her way across the heaving deck.

"You're one of the sailors, aren't you?" she said.

He looked down at her and nodded, without smiling.

"Please. I need some help terribly. Dad's lying on the floor of his cabin and I can't get him back into his bunk." She started back across the salon, clinging to upset chairs to steady herself against the pitch and roll of the *Bonito*.

Sherman followed her, scorning handholds. He saw her step into the first cabin and he looked in through the door. Herbert Marmion lay sprawled miserably on the littered rug. Sherman stepped through and encircled the man's body with strong arms. Without seeming effort, he picked the man up and shoved him into the bunk. The man lay there, moaning.

Suddenly the fat-rimmed eyes started wide and the soft, plump hands clawed at Bob's slicker.

"Are we going to sink?"

"How should I know? Ask that two-for-a-nickel captain of yours!" Sherman swung around and went back into the passageway, Herbert Marmion's panicky cries following him.

The girl followed Sherman out and closed the door. She looked up at the sailor, a troubled expression in her eyes. She tugged at his arm. Bringing her mouth close to his ear, she said, "Who are you?"

"You wouldn't be interested." Sherman stared hard at her for a moment. "Who's next?" he said abruptly.

The girl frowned and led down the passageway to a pantry. She stepped in, making her way around broken dishes and dented pans. Picking up a copper coffeepot, she made a

93

helpless gesture in the direction of the door. Sherman entered and looked about. He saw a small oil stove and a water tappet. Pointing to a can of coffee lashed on the shelf, he applied a match to the stove and stood back, watching the blue flame lick around the wick.

The girl handed him the filled pot. Bob lashed two towels around the handle and spout, and tied it on the stove. He glanced back and saw that the girl had seated herself on a built-in table and was quietly considering him. He noted with indifference that she was beautiful. Her hair was swept back from her forehead and was glisteningly jet-black. Her eyes were almost as dark as her hair. Yes, Sherman thought, she showed more beauty and breeding than he would have expected in a Marmion.

The coffee was boiling, and Sherman wrapped the towels around it and picked it up. The girl took several heavy cups from the debris on the floor and led the way back up the passage. But no one wanted coffee—neither the girl's father and mother, nor Percy Gilman, her fiancé, nor any of the Marmions' friends.

The girl and Sherman went back to the pantry. He set the coffee pot in a corner where the contents wouldn't spill, and, at the girl's invitation, sat down on the built-in table. Then he saw that a ventilator above was letting spray down upon them and he closed it. He kicked the pantry doors shut and found that he had blotted out the sound of the raging hurricane. The girl poured out two cups of coffee, and they sat down on the table again.

The girl was staring across the narrow pantry at a fragment of china, nursing the warmth of the cup in her two slender hands.

"I don't blame you for being a swashbuckler, Bob."

Sherman started and spilled some of his coffee.

"How did you know my name?"

The girl smiled.

To find out more about *Sea Fangs* and how you can obtain your copy, go to www.goldenagestories.com.

Glossary

Glossary

STORIES FROM THE GOLDEN AGE *reflect the words and expressions used in the 1930s and 1940s, adding unique flavor and authenticity to the tales. While a character's speech may often reflect regional origins, it also can convey attitudes common in the day. So that readers can better grasp such cultural and historical terms, uncommon words or expressions of the era, the following glossary has been provided.*

---

ballast tanks: tanks in the bottom and sides of a submarine that are flooded with sea water, making the submarine heavier and permitting it to descend beneath the surface of the sea. When the submarine is ready to come to the surface, air is pumped into the ballast tanks, which pushes out the water through vents and makes the submarine light enough to rise.

bead on, take a: to take careful aim at. This term alludes to the bead, a small metal knob on a firearm used as a front sight.

"bears": from the phrase "come bear a hand," which means to lend a hand or bring your hand to bear on the work going on. Bears refer to those who are helping.

belaying pin: a large wooden or metal pin that fits into a hole in a rail on a ship or boat, and to which a rope can be fastened.

bends, the: a condition caused by a rapid substantial decrease in atmospheric pressure when coming up from deep-sea diving, characterized by the formation of nitrogen bubbles in the blood and severe pain in the lungs and joints.

binnacle: a built-in housing for a ship's compass.

bitt: a vertical post, usually one of a pair, set on the deck of a ship and used for securing cables, lines for towing, etc.

bone in the teeth: said of a ship speeding along throwing up spray or foam under the bow. The phrase comes from the image of a dog, merrily running with a bone in its teeth.

Ciudad de Oro: (Spanish) City of Gold.

cock-and-bull story: a tale so full of improbable details and embellishments that it is obviously not true.

Colt .45: a .45-caliber automatic pistol manufactured by the Colt Firearms Company of Hartford, Connecticut. Colt was founded in 1847 by Samuel Colt (1814–1862), who revolutionized the firearms industry.

corselet: part of a diver's suit consisting of a breastplate made of copper or iron, shaped so that it fits comfortably over the shoulders, chest and back. Once in place, the corselet is bolted to the suit and the diving helmet is then locked onto the corselet.

cutlass: a short, heavy, slightly curved sword with a single cutting edge, formerly used by sailors.

diving piano: the name given to the collection of levers in a submarine's control room that operate the diving and resurfacing mechanisms.

dogs: any of various hooked or U-shaped metallic devices used for holding, gripping or fastening.

fathom: a unit of length equal to six feet (1.83 meters), used in measuring the depth of water.

galleon: a large three-masted sailing ship, usually with two or more decks; used mainly by the Spanish from the fifteenth to eighteenth centuries for war and commerce.

gangway: a narrow, movable platform or ramp forming a bridge by which to board or leave a ship.

G-men: government men; agents of the Federal Bureau of Investigation.

grandstand play: a showy action or move, as in a sport, in order to gain attention or approval.

Haiti: country in the Caribbean occupying the western part of the island of Hispaniola. The other half is occupied by the Dominican Republic.

halyard: a rope used for raising and lowering a sail.

hawser: a thick rope or cable for mooring or towing a ship.

jackstaff: a flagstaff at the bow of a vessel, on which a small national flag, known as a jack, is flown.

Jacob's ladder: a hanging ladder having ropes or chains supporting wooden or metal rungs or steps.

lungs: underwater breathing apparatuses. Between 1929 and 1932, two US naval officers developed a Submarine Escape Lung that consisted of an oblong rubber bag that recycled exhaled air. Called the "Momsen Lung" after the name of one of the officers, it hung around the neck and strapped around the waist and allowed for slow ascent to avoid the bends.

out on my feet: in a state of being unconscious or senseless but still being on one's feet—standing up.

painter: a rope, usually at the bow, for fastening a boat to a ship, stake, etc.

plate: precious metal.

pulmotor: a mechanical device for artificial respiration that forces oxygen into the lungs when respiration has ceased because of drowning, etc.

quintal: a unit of weight equal to one hundred pounds.

Scheherazade: the female narrator of *The Arabian Nights*, who during one thousand and one adventurous nights saved her life by entertaining her husband, the king, with stories.

scuppers: openings in the side of a ship at deck level that allow water to run off.

stand on and off: to keep at a safe distance; to sail alternately toward and away from shore so as to keep a point in sight.

sweeps: long, heavy oars.

thwarts: seats across a boat, especially those used by rowers.

tin fish: a submarine.

tramp steamer: a freight vessel that does not run regularly between fixed ports, but takes a cargo wherever shippers desire.

transom: transom seat; a kind of bench seat, usually with a locker or drawers underneath.

truck: a piece of wood fixed at the top of the highest mast on a ship, usually having holes through which ropes can be passed to raise or lower sails or flags.

under weigh: in motion; underway.

weather eye open, keep a: to be on one's guard; be watchful.

weigh anchor: take up the anchor when ready to sail.

West Indies: a group of islands in the North Atlantic between North and South America, comprising the Greater Antilles, the Lesser Antilles and the Bahamas.

Windward Passage: a channel between Haiti and Cuba that connects the Atlantic Ocean with the Caribbean Sea.

L. Ron Hubbard
in the Golden Age
of Pulp Fiction

*In writing an adventure story
a writer has to know that he is adventuring
for a lot of people who cannot.
The writer has to take them here and there
about the globe and show them
excitement and love and realism.
As long as that writer is living the part of an
adventurer when he is hammering
the keys, he is succeeding with his story.*

*Adventuring is a state of mind.
If you adventure through life, you have a
good chance to be a success on paper.*

*Adventure doesn't mean globe-trotting,
exactly, and it doesn't mean great deeds.
Adventuring is like art.
You have to live it to make it real.*

—L. RON HUBBARD

L. Ron Hubbard
and American
Pulp Fiction

BORN March 13, 1911, L. Ron Hubbard lived a life at least as expansive as the stories with which he enthralled a hundred million readers through a fifty-year career.

Originally hailing from Tilden, Nebraska, he spent his formative years in a classically rugged Montana, replete with the cowpunchers, lawmen and desperadoes who would later people his Wild West adventures. And lest anyone imagine those adventures were drawn from vicarious experience, he was not only breaking broncs at a tender age, he was also among the few whites ever admitted into Blackfoot society as a bona fide blood brother. While if only to round out an otherwise rough and tumble youth, his mother was that rarity of her time—a thoroughly educated woman—who introduced her son to the classics of Occidental literature even before his seventh birthday.

But as any dedicated L. Ron Hubbard reader will attest, his world extended far beyond Montana. In point of fact, and as the son of a United States naval officer, by the age of eighteen he had traveled over a quarter of a million miles. Included therein were three Pacific crossings to a then still mysterious Asia, where he ran with the likes of Her British Majesty's agent-in-place

L. Ron Hubbard, left, at Congressional Airport, Washington, DC, 1931, with members of George Washington University flying club.

for North China, and the last in the line of Royal Magicians from the court of Kublai Khan. For the record, L. Ron Hubbard was also among the first Westerners to gain admittance to forbidden Tibetan monasteries below Manchuria, and his photographs of China's Great Wall long graced American geography texts.

Upon his return to the United States and a hasty completion of his interrupted high school education, the young Ron Hubbard entered George Washington University. There, as fans of his aerial adventures may have heard, he earned his wings as a pioneering barnstormer at the dawn of American aviation. He also earned a place in free-flight record books for the longest sustained flight above Chicago. Moreover, as a roving reporter for *Sportsman Pilot* (featuring his first professionally penned articles), he further helped inspire a generation of pilots who would take America to world airpower.

Immediately beyond his sophomore year, Ron embarked on the first of his famed ethnological expeditions, initially to then untrammeled Caribbean shores (descriptions of which would later fill a whole series of West Indies mystery-thrillers). That the Puerto Rican interior would also figure into the future of Ron Hubbard stories was likewise no accident. For in addition to cultural studies of the island, a 1932–33

LRH expedition is rightly remembered as conducting the first complete mineralogical survey of a Puerto Rico under United States jurisdiction.

There was many another adventure along this vein: As a lifetime member of the famed Explorers Club, L. Ron Hubbard charted North Pacific waters with the first shipboard radio direction finder, and so pioneered a long-range navigation system universally employed until the late twentieth century. While not to put too fine an edge on it, he also held a rare Master Mariner's license to pilot any vessel, of any tonnage in any ocean.

Yet lest we stray too far afield, there is an LRH note at this juncture in his saga, and it reads in part:

"I started out writing for the pulps, writing the best I knew, writing for every mag on the stands, slanting as well as I could."

To which one might add: His earliest submissions date from the summer of 1934, and included tales drawn from true-to-life Asian adventures, with characters roughly modeled on British/American intelligence operatives he had known in Shanghai. His early Westerns were similarly peppered with details drawn from personal experience. Although therein lay a first hard lesson from the often cruel world of the pulps. His first Westerns were soundly rejected as lacking the authenticity of a Max Brand yarn

Capt. L. Ron Hubbard in Ketchikan, Alaska, 1940, on his Alaskan Radio Experimental Expedition, the first of three voyages conducted under the Explorers Club flag.

(a particularly frustrating comment given L. Ron Hubbard's Westerns came straight from his Montana homeland, while Max Brand was a mediocre New York poet named Frederick Schiller Faust, who turned out implausible six-shooter tales from the terrace of an Italian villa).

Nevertheless, and needless to say, L. Ron Hubbard persevered and soon earned a reputation as among the most publishable names in pulp fiction, with a ninety percent placement rate of first-draft manuscripts. He was also among the most prolific, averaging between seventy and a hundred thousand words a month. Hence the rumors that L. Ron Hubbard had redesigned a typewriter for faster keyboard action and pounded out manuscripts on a continuous roll of butcher paper to save the precious seconds it took to insert a single sheet of paper into manual typewriters of the day.

That all L. Ron Hubbard stories did not run beneath said byline is yet another aspect of pulp fiction lore. That is, as publishers periodically rejected manuscripts from top-drawer authors if only to avoid paying top dollar, L. Ron Hubbard and company just as frequently replied with submissions under various pseudonyms. In Ron's case, the list

A MAN OF MANY NAMES

Between 1934 and 1950, L. Ron Hubbard authored more than fifteen million words of fiction in more than two hundred classic publications. To supply his fans and editors with stories across an array of genres and pulp titles, he adopted fifteen pseudonyms in addition to his already renowned L. Ron Hubbard byline.

Winchester Remington Colt
Lt. Jonathan Daly
Capt. Charles Gordon
Capt. L. Ron Hubbard
Bernard Hubbel
Michael Keith
Rene Lafayette
Legionnaire 148
Legionnaire 14830
Ken Martin
Scott Morgan
Lt. Scott Morgan
Kurt von Rachen
Barry Randolph
Capt. Humbert Reynolds

included: Rene Lafayette, Captain Charles Gordon, Lt. Scott Morgan and the notorious Kurt von Rachen—supposedly on the lam for a murder rap, while hammering out two-fisted prose in Argentina. The point: While L. Ron Hubbard as Ken Martin spun stories of Southeast Asian intrigue, LRH as Barry Randolph authored tales of

L. Ron Hubbard, circa 1930, at the outset of a literary career that would finally span half a century.

romance on the Western range—which, stretching between a dozen genres is how he came to stand among the two hundred elite authors providing close to a million tales through the glory days of American Pulp Fiction.

In evidence of exactly that, by 1936 L. Ron Hubbard was literally leading pulp fiction's elite as president of New York's American Fiction Guild. Members included a veritable pulp hall of fame: Lester "Doc Savage" Dent, Walter "The Shadow" Gibson, and the legendary Dashiell Hammett—to cite but a few.

Also in evidence of just where L. Ron Hubbard stood within his first two years on the American pulp circuit: By the spring of 1937, he was ensconced in Hollywood, adopting a Caribbean thriller for Columbia Pictures, remembered today as *The Secret of Treasure Island.* Comprising fifteen thirty-minute episodes, the L. Ron Hubbard screenplay led to the most profitable matinée serial in Hollywood history. In accord with Hollywood culture, he was thereafter continually called

The 1937 Secret of Treasure Island, *a fifteen-episode serial adapted for the screen by L. Ron Hubbard from his novel,* Murder at Pirate Castle.

upon to rewrite/doctor scripts—most famously for long-time friend and fellow adventurer Clark Gable.

In the interim—and herein lies another distinctive chapter of the L. Ron Hubbard story—he continually worked to open Pulp Kingdom gates to up-and-coming authors. Or, for that matter, anyone who wished to write. It was a fairly unconventional stance, as markets were already thin and competition razor sharp. But the fact remains, it was an L. Ron Hubbard hallmark that he vehemently lobbied on behalf of young authors—regularly supplying instructional articles to trade journals, guest-lecturing to short story classes at George Washington University and Harvard, and even founding his own creative writing competition. It was established in 1940, dubbed the Golden Pen, and guaranteed winners both New York representation and publication in *Argosy.*

But it was John W. Campbell Jr.'s *Astounding Science Fiction* that finally proved the most memorable LRH vehicle. While every fan of L. Ron Hubbard's galactic epics undoubtedly knows the story, it nonetheless bears repeating: By late 1938, the pulp publishing magnate of Street & Smith was determined to revamp *Astounding Science Fiction* for broader readership. In particular, senior editorial director F. Orlin Tremaine called for stories with a stronger *human element.* When acting editor John W. Campbell balked, preferring his spaceship-driven tales,

Tremaine enlisted Hubbard. Hubbard, in turn, replied with the genre's first truly *character-driven* works, wherein heroes are pitted not against bug-eyed monsters but the mystery and majesty of deep space itself—and thus was launched the Golden Age of Science Fiction.

The names alone are enough to quicken the pulse of any science fiction aficionado, including LRH friend and protégé, Robert Heinlein, Isaac Asimov, A. E. van Vogt and Ray Bradbury. Moreover, when coupled with LRH stories of fantasy, we further come to what's rightly been described as the

foundation of every modern tale of horror: L. Ron Hubbard's immortal *Fear*. It was rightly proclaimed by Stephen King as one of the very few works to genuinely warrant that overworked term "classic"—as in: *"This is a classic tale of creeping, surreal menace and horror. . . . This is one of the really, really good ones."*

To accommodate the greater body of L. Ron Hubbard fantasies, Street & Smith inaugurated *Unknown*—a classic pulp if there ever was one, and wherein readers were soon thrilling to the likes of *Typewriter in the Sky* and *Slaves of Sleep* of which Frederik Pohl would declare: *"There are bits and pieces from Ron's work that became part of the language in ways that very few other writers managed."*

L. Ron Hubbard, 1948, among fellow science fiction luminaries at the World Science Fiction Convention in Toronto.

And, indeed, at J. W. Campbell Jr.'s insistence, Ron was regularly drawing on themes from the Arabian Nights and so introducing readers to a world of genies, jinn, Aladdin and Sinbad—all of which, of course, continue to float through cultural mythology to this day.

At least as influential in terms of post-apocalypse stories was L. Ron Hubbard's 1940 *Final Blackout*. Generally acclaimed as the finest anti-war novel of the decade and among the ten best works of the genre ever authored—here, too, was a tale that would live on in ways few other writers imagined. Hence, the later Robert Heinlein verdict: "Final Blackout *is as perfect a piece of science fiction as has ever been written."*

Like many another who both lived and wrote American pulp adventure, the war proved a tragic end to Ron's sojourn in the pulps. He served with distinction in four theaters and was highly decorated for commanding corvettes in the North Pacific. He was also grievously wounded in combat, lost many a close friend and colleague and thus resolved to say farewell to pulp fiction and devote himself to what it had supported these many years—namely, his serious research.

Portland, Oregon, 1943; L. Ron Hubbard captain of the US Navy subchaser PC 815.

But in no way was the LRH literary saga at an end, for as he wrote some thirty years later, in 1980:

"Recently there came a period when I had little to do. This was novel in a life so crammed with busy years, and I decided to amuse myself by writing a novel that was pure science fiction."

That work was *Battlefield Earth: A Saga of the Year 3000*. It was an immediate *New York Times* bestseller and, in fact, the first international science fiction blockbuster in decades. It was not, however, L. Ron Hubbard's magnum opus, as that distinction is generally reserved for his next and final work: The 1.2 million word *Mission Earth*.

> **Final Blackout**
> *is as perfect a piece of science fiction as has ever been written.*
>
> —Robert Heinlein

How he managed those 1.2 million words in just over twelve months is yet another piece of the L. Ron Hubbard legend. But the fact remains, he did indeed author a ten-volume *dekalogy* that lives in publishing history for the fact that each and every volume of the series was also a *New York Times* bestseller.

Moreover, as subsequent generations discovered L. Ron Hubbard through republished works and novelizations of his screenplays, the mere fact of his name on a cover signaled an international bestseller. . . . Until, to date, sales of his works exceed hundreds of millions, and he otherwise remains among the most enduring and widely read authors in literary history. Although as a final word on the tales of L. Ron Hubbard, perhaps it's enough to simply reiterate what editors told readers in the glory days of American Pulp Fiction:

He writes the way he does, brothers, because he's been there, seen it and done it!

THE STORIES FROM THE GOLDEN AGE

Your ticket to adventure starts here with the Stories from
the Golden Age collection by master storyteller L. Ron Hubbard.
These gripping tales are set in a kaleidoscope of exotic locales and brim
with fascinating characters, including some of the
most vile villains, dangerous dames and brazen heroes
you'll ever get to meet.

The entire collection of over one hundred and fifty stories is being
released in a series of eighty books and audiobooks.
For an up-to-date listing of available titles,
go to www.goldenagestories.com.

AIR ADVENTURE

Arctic Wings   *Man-Killers of the Air*
The Battling Pilot   *On Blazing Wings*
Boomerang Bomber   *Red Death Over China*
The Crate Killer   *Sabotage in the Sky*
The Dive Bomber   *Sky Birds Dare!*
Forbidden Gold   *The Sky-Crasher*
Hurtling Wings   *Trouble on His Wings*
The Lieutenant Takes the Sky   *Wings Over Ethiopia*

FAR-FLUNG ADVENTURE

SEA ADVENTURE

TALES FROM THE ORIENT

MYSTERY

FANTASY

Borrowed Glory   *If I Were You*
The Crossroads   *The Last Drop*
Danger in the Dark   *The Room*
The Devil's Rescue   *The Tramp*
He Didn't Like Cats

SCIENCE FICTION

The Automagic Horse   *A Matter of Matter*
Battle of Wizards   *The Obsolete Weapon*
Battling Bolto   *One Was Stubborn*
The Beast   *The Planet Makers*
Beyond All Weapons   *The Professor Was a Thief*
A Can of Vacuum   *The Slaver*
The Conroy Diary   *Space Can*
The Dangerous Dimension *Strain*
Final Enemy   *Tough Old Man*
The Great Secret   *240,000 Miles Straight Up*
Greed   *When Shadows Fall*
The Invaders

120

WESTERN